TRAVELING WITH ATHENA

TRAVELING WITH ATHENA

A Blind Man's Odyssey through Italy and Greece

Daniel Pukstas

iUniverse, Inc.
New York Lincoln Shanghai

Traveling with Athena

A Blind Man's Odyssey through Italy and Greece

iUniverse, Inc.

For information address:
iUniverse, Inc.
2021 Pine Lake Road, Suite 100
Lincoln, NE 68512
www.iuniverse.com

ISBN: 0-595-27943-0

Printed in the United States of America

For Nancy

C O N T E N T S

▼

Acknowledgments

Special thanks go to Laura Tate who typed the original manuscript of this book. Zeus must have sent Hermes to help her decipher my scrawl. Additional gratitude goes to Robin Hinchcliff, who edited the initial draft with me. Her patience, perspicacity, and laughter made a difficult task delightful.

Introduction

As a child I was fascinated by the movie Ulysses and the wonderful portrayal Kirk Douglas provided of this mighty hero. The battle with the Cyclops and Ulysses' bloody triumph over the suitors captured my imagination and my soul. I longed to be part of such an adventure, to have such a journey.

As I grew older I never fully abandoned the idea that I would some day make a special journey, an odyssey of my own. However, when my eyesight degenerated to the level of legal blindness in 1994, the role for which I had been cast seemed more to be that of the blind seer Tiresias than the great adventurer Ulysses (Odysseus). And so, with resignation, I put the flickering flame of my fantasy in a remote recess of my brain where I knew it would eventually burn itself out though I had no desire to snuff it out quickly or purposely.

In 1999, however, a marvelous thing happened. I listened to a recording of Robert Fagles' translation of Homer's Iliad. This was followed by Fagles' translation of The Odyssey. The flame no longer flickered; it blazed. Furthermore, as if ordained by Zeus himself, I was soon to be eligible for a semester sabbatic leave. The gods smiled on me, and I was granted time off from my teaching position to study the classics and travel to Greece and Italy, the lands of classical epic.

In The Odyssey Odysseus does not succeed on his own. Though he is courageous, clever, and a great warrior, he would have been defeated on many occasions and drowned in the wine-dark seas were it not for the intercession of the goddess Athena. She advocates to Zeus for Odysseus, guides and advises him, takes on disguises to help him— even fights at his side. Odysseus did have his Penelope, but she was a destination, not a fellow traveler. I was more fortunate than Odysseus. My wife Nancy would travel with me. On many occasions she would bear the burden of heroism.

Yet, luckier than Odysseus in that I had my wife's company, I was less fortunate in that I also had my visual disability. For my journey to be successful I would need additional help. Perhaps because she has a special place in her heart for mortals who are risk-takers and who revere her, Athena smiled on me and took me on as one of her children. Her presence in our journey seems undeniable as the tale of our travels will certainly reveal.

If travel helps to form a person, to help him grow and evolve, then the account of a journey needs to be more than a collection of geographical locations and the best places to get a good deal. This account will, of course, discuss the external elements of the journey, but, more importantly, it will record the wanderings of my thoughts. At times I hope the reader will find these thoughts amusing and entertaining; at other times I hope they will be exciting, and in a few cases I hope the reader will find my observations insightful.

At the end of the journey the reader will know me as a person, just as we know Odysseus at the end of Homer's great tale. The reader will also admire Nancy and wonder at her courage. And, lastly, the reader will rethink the existence of the gods as my story demonstrates again and again the intervention of a goddess as Nancy and I go traveling with Athena.

Daniel J. Pukstas
Cortland, New York

Invocation

Inspire me, O Muse,
That I may sing
Of modern-day prodigious
wanderings.
Teach me to best reveal
Athena's generous aid and gracious
weal
To one who journeys full deprived
of sight
And his fair dame who scaled
bravery's height.
Anoint the words and phrases that
I use,
So that my readers of this book
May amuse,
Or capture them with revelations
Keen.

CHAPTER I

▼

ODYSSEUS WOULDN'T HAVE MADE IT AS A TRAVEL AGENT

For a moment I had no idea where I was—or for that matter, who I was—as the "Fasten Your Seat Belts" bell woke me from a drooling, head-bobbing nap of perhaps five minutes. I had felt worse than this, but I certainly wasn't savoring the mild headache, churning stomach, strained neck, and overall bodily discomfort that are all part of an overseas flight. The airline captains routinely suggest that we passengers "sit back and enjoy the flight." What an amazingly disingenuous thing to say! It's like a dentist suggesting that we sit back and enjoy the latest in oral technology.

Yet, there are positive things to consider about modern air travel. Nearly forty years after its initial rollout, the Boeing 747 is still an impressive achievement. Forget the design; just putting all the pieces together boggles my mind. When I witness the incredible ineptness of people boarding the plane, I wonder how any human activity ever gets done. In the Tower of Babel boarding process, apparently everyone is a person with small children or special needs. Evidently, anyone who had the potential to participate in the conception of a small child or who has had a hand in the conception process at some point feels full entitlement to rush the boarding checkpoint. The only group left out would be infertile virgins. These are obviously people with special needs, so everyone is included. This, of course, means that as people board the plane, all the aisles are blocked by those storing their prolific carry-on items which have magically multiplied to three or four per person despite the airline's warning that only one item of the smallest size will be allowed. I slide my small carry-on under the seat in front of me and feel like a fool. If my luggage is lost, I'll be wearing the same underwear for a week and brushing my teeth with my finger. And yet, from such a humanity that conjures chaos from the simple act of boarding comes an assembled machine of a million parts that can fly at 500 miles per hour! I'd better stop thinking about it; it scares me.

As I begin to recover from my mini-nap, I'm struck by the fact that this plane is carrying about the same number of people who sailed in the twelve ships of Odysseus, one of the world's most famous travelers. As a tour guide, Odysseus wouldn't have lasted long. First of all, it took him ten years to make it from Troy to Ithaca. Even with really bad connections, this seems a bit too long. Secondly, and perhaps more importantly, Odysseus didn't get anyone but himself back home. Sure, a number of his group had pretty exciting finishes. A half dozen were snatched from deck by the six-headed Scylla; a few more were fin-ger-food for Polyphemus, the giant Cyclops. Others were changed to animals, changed back again, and then drowned. "Wait 'til I tell the gang at the office what happened to me" is something we all want to bring back from a trip, but at the end of the Odyssey tours only Odys-seus was left talking. It's a good thing he was a king; he never would have made it in the travel business.

At this point the muse saw that the beverage cart was no longer blocking the aisle to the restroom so she left. Now, there are those who might think I'm being facetious or cute by assigning restroom requirements to a goddess, but this is not the case. Anyone who reads the classics knows that the gods are caught up in bodily functions. The famous classical writers, however, knew that the bodily function of sexual appetite would be most appealing to audiences, so they concentrated on it. Zeus, of course, leads the league here, and his kinky dress-up tricks have no parallel in literature. He played the game of love as a bull, a swan—even a shower of coins. It's easy to see why he was king of the gods. Food also plays a prominent role in the lives of the gods. How much more could have been accomplished by mortal heroes if they did not spend so much time setting up slaughters of farm animals and the follow-up barbecues to satisfy the sacrificial demands of the apparently tapeworm infested gods. Now, all this chow has to go somewhere. The bards of the past, however, different from the sophisticated writers of the present did not think that divine dignity would be served by the poesy of the pot, so they merely had the gods excuse themselves without much ado or specificity. Those familiar with the works of Homer, Virgil, Aristophanes, and the rest know that gods and goddesses are always popping in and out of the action. Blink an eye for a second as a page is turned, and Athena disappears. Where did she go? Most probably to the loo.

In any event, with the departure of my muse, I was forced to analyze the many modern mysteries of modern air travel without inspiration and all by myself. The first developed from the fact that throughout my seven-hour flight there were always movies, cartoons, television programs, and documentaries on the screen for viewing. Well, what's mysterious about this? The mystery is that this wasn't always the case. For decades, even though the technology allowed it, airlines would schedule one movie to be the sole entertainment for the entire flight. Even more mysterious is the fact that the airlines would charge for this diversion. Hadn't they ever heard of "the opiate of the masses"? Since I am legally blind, I can't participate in such diversions and let me say without hesitation that we all need to be diverted when sitting in seats designed for someone 62% of our size!

The second mystery of air travel involves those very seats. Why is it that the first person in every row to thrust back her seat—usually to the most horizontal position possible—is the smallest person in the row? And the beauty of the thrust is that there is absolutely no concern for the comfort or kneecaps of the person in the seat behind. Of course, this first recliner sets off the "kick the cat" syndrome in which each passenger takes out his anger for the person in the seat in front of him by punishing the passenger behind him—in spades!

The final mystery is one I wish to take up with the National Institute of Health. How can there be so many more people with colds boarding an aircraft than there are on average in the general population when aircraft passengers are generally more affluent and better fed (when they're not on the airplane) than the general population? In fact, the percentage of colds seems almost as high as it is among teenagers who actually seem to pursue the acquisition of colds as a kind of status symbol. After all, what else would account for their avoidance of proper clothing in winter such as hats and coats, their refusal to sleep, and their increased libido when confronted with a partner who is obviously at the ripest and most contagious part of a cold?

My infectious statistic was a woman of fifty. She was quite ripe with her cold although I did not feel any compulsion to kiss her in either a French or English style. She knew she was infected and gave me and my wife little cellophane packages of lifesavers. I knew this cellophane was covered with germs, but I fatalistically accepted it. The cold was a sure thing. I got it 72 hours later.

Yet, somehow I was blessed. The cold turned out to be quite mild. Although it made me conscious I have a nose (since I can't see it in the mirror, I don't think much about it), it didn't become the center of my universe as can happen when an intense cold strikes. Then a facial appendage of only a few inches can seem like the Rock of Gibralter in a hurricane during a cannonade. Amid torrents of water, great bursts of wind and hellish material explode outward. I, however, only needed one small tissue, and in light of the suffering endured by those traveling in Odysseus tour groups, I really had nothing to complain about.

CHAPTER 2

▼

POSEIDON'S REVENGE

People often ask me about the difficulties and disappointments of being blind. Certainly the inability to see my lovely wife and two children and to experience the world of natural beauty would have to be included in my losses. In addition, the inability to read is an artistic and intellectual deprivation that strikes me deeply. However, along with this list is a difficulty of the most basic kind—the problem of using public restrooms.

Toilets are for the sighted. Their layout, cleanliness, plumbing, and protocol are all presented through visual cues. Even in the United States a public restroom is a challenging experience. In countries where I did not speak the native language, I dreaded regularity. Now some might wonder about the other senses that blind people are supposed to be so clever to use. Well, taste is obviously out of the question. Hearing can be used to determine water flow and the presence of strangers. Smell can reveal cleanliness and perhaps the recent application of sanitizing chemicals. But when all is said and done, where is the necessary ceramic equipment? Only touch can tell us. Oh, how I hope there's soap in the dispensers!

It's become fashionable in American intellectual circles to celebrate diversity. However, I have to part company with this crowd on the issue of bathroom equipment and design. Can't we standardize this stuff! Stalls are placed to the left, to the right, in front, and in back. Ceramic sinks and urinals take turns on the left of the room and the right. Soap dispensers are hung just over the sink or high up on a perpendicular wall. How about those push dispensers next to the faucets that always seem to be empty! Paper towels are the worst. They're so badly placed that I have given up looking for them. I dry my hands on my pants and my wife's sweater.

Now this diversity is a problem in the U. S.; in Europe it's a disaster. The European community will start using a single currency in 2002. When this trivial matter is handled, I hope they develop a uniform protocol for toilet uniformity next. First, let's agree that sitting is better than squatting. Toilet seat pregnancies aside, I'm not worried about bottom to bottom germ dispersal. I am, however, terrified of sticking my cane—or my foot—into the hole in the floor that passes for a toilet. I know that this style has a long cultural tradition; the same could be said of slavery. It's time for a holy war to eliminate this option. By the way, I'm not open to compromise here. Some places have a ceramic bowl with no seat. One sits on the edge of the enamel. Clearly, this leads to nothing but soggy pants and pantyhose.

Once we install the seated toilet, a United Nations protocol might develop a universal placement for the flushing mechanism. Currently, there are foot pedals, covered floor buttons, pull chains, wall buttons, real handles, tank buttons, plastic wall panels, etc. Why not add secret compartments to this list! We have such a long way to go in this area of human activity.

But as a blind traveler, I live in the present. How do I manage? It's simple; I dehydrate myself. Now, I know that authorities say that to avoid jet lag, one should drink a half gallon of water every four minutes. However, I've heard the restroom rage from those standing in the aisles of aircraft. It's a simple choice: rage or jet lag. I've chosen the latter, and I'm proud to say that I have never used an aircraft bathroom—even on international flights!

Using the airport restrooms, however, is another story, and here's where Poseidon's Revenge comes in. Like many of the gods, Poseidon, god of the sea, produced unusual children. Polyphemus was one of these. Polyphemus was a giant Cyclops who was a herdsman on an island visited by Odysseus and his men. Unfortunately, Polyphemus had a strange concept of hospitality—he ate his guests! Odysseus, of course, had to escape from this fee, fi, fo, fum fiefdom and wound up burning out Polyphemus' one great eye. Poseidon didn't care for this treatment of his son and made Odysseus' journey over the water very difficult. I also believe that after this event Poseidon developed an irrational dislike of blind people and the subject of blindness because it made him think of his son and caused him unhappiness. It was this irrational response to Poseidon that caught up to me at Milan's Malpensa Airport.

I should hardly have been surprised to find difficulty at an airport named Malpensa; its literal meaning sounds like "bad thoughts" or "evil thinking." In any event, when I landed I had a need for a restroom. Malpensa is a new airport, and I hoped for the best. However, when I entered the men's room, there seemed to be a problem. The first stall door had a piece of paper attached to it. It might have said "Welcome to Hell," but more likely it said in Italian, "Out of Order." I moved slowly down the group of stalls, heard some flushing water, and then found an open stall door. I proceeded in and closed the door behind me. At this point I noticed Poseidon's work. I was standing in an inch of water. In addition, there was no seat on the ceramic toilet. I didn't bother to look for the flushing mechanism. I couldn't use this facility. I had flown over Poseidon's empire in the plane. But here in the water closet Poseidon had exacted his irrational revenge. I headed for the restroom exit, sloshing through what seemed to be an incoming and rising tide. I wondered if this was the beginning of weeks of watery wandering through the restrooms of the Mediterranean.

Seeing my despair, Athena, taking the form of my wife Nancy, guided me to another bank of restrooms where, mirabile dictu (literally, "wondrous to say"), there was a single restroom dedicated for handicapped use only! Athena guarded the door. Toilet paper and soap were available and I found a flushing button on the wall. Poseidon gnashed his teeth.

Nancy and I would look for such restrooms for the disabled at all of our stops. Sometimes we'd find them; at other times we weren't so lucky. When we were fortunate, however, Nancy could bring me into the room and show me where all the critical fixtures and handles were located. On these days I would dedicate a glass of wine to Athena for helping us against Poseidon.

CHAPTER 3

▼

REX AND ARGUS

Unconditional love—it's something humans have always longed for. For conditional love we're ready to trade much; it's no surprise then that for unconditional love we're ready to become irrational, emotional, and hyperbolic. This is obviously found in the one creature who can give any one of us unconditional love—the dog. Because it will love us without question—something no other creature can do—we've assigned it cult status. Show a picture of a puppy, and the world oohs and ahs. Harm a dog, and the cries for justice and punishment drown out those hurled at a mass murderer.

The publicity about dogs is one-sided. When a dog saves a human life, the event is trumpeted over the headlines for days. No such equal press goes to the hundreds of thousands of cases where people are sent to the emergency room because of dog bites. I would also bet that more lives are lost by people trying to save dogs than are actually saved by dogs, but there's not much press appeal to this aspect of devotion to dogs.

But, as I say, the cult of the canine is neither rational nor statistically analytical, and in the Western Tradition it has transcended millennia and national boundaries. In Homer's Odyssey, for example, one of the most touching scenes of the entire epic occurs when—after twenty years—Argus, Odysseus' dog, sees and recognizes his master, even though Odysseus is in disguise. Argus is lying on a dung heap. After his moment of recognition, he dies. Few readers are not touched by this scene of canine loyalty.

The Mediterranean world still abounds in this tradition. In France in 1973 I remember seeing a French woman walking her dog on the very top of the Pont du Gard Aqueduct, a rough surface several hundred feet above the stream below. I was so terrified of falling myself that I crept on the surface on my hands and knees. However, this woman—in high heels to boot—strode along with her little dog as if she were strolling along the Champs Elysee.

When I visited Spain for five months it was clear that the Spanish had a bad case of cynophilia. Dogs and their droppings were everywhere. The Spanish also tend to favor the larger dogs. Nancy and I were able to empathize with the matadors of the bullfight as we dealt with these large—and often unleashed—animals. Nancy will never forget one incident in particular when a large dog jumped a fence at eye level right in front of her.

The Italians also suffer from puppy love, and they bring their dogs to work. Several four-star hotels we visited seemed to have dogs as part of the staff. They would escort us from our car into the lobby area and then resume their door man's post up front. One even followed us to the door of our room even though we took the elevator, and he didn't!

Sometimes dogs seem to be owned by a district rather than an individual. Rex of Gheti in Chianti was such an individual. Everyone seemed to know him, and he seemed at home with everyone. Other dogs in the area were quite territorial. Rex was king of all he surveyed. Rex was also different in how he handled his preeminence. Where other dogs were anxious and insistent in their efforts to be top dog with barking, growling, and posturing, Rex just couldn't be bothered. When Nancy and I first met him, he threw himself upon his back and exposed his stomach for pats and strokes. I'm told that this is a submissive posture for dogs, but Rex had learned a simple truth that many people—especially disabled ones—often fail to learn: one gains control by giving up control. Rex had delegated his care and feeding to a community of others; as a result he had become King of Chianti.

I met other dogs who have taken the same enlightened approach to life and have abandoned the ferocious hurling of self against fences and the intimidating death-growling for a much more fulfilling existence. On Isola de Pescadores (sounds much better than Fisherman's Island) in Lago Maggiore, another royal dog snoozed in the middle of the street as scores of tourists gave him proper courtesy and bumped and jostled each other rather than disturb this lordly animal. At the top of the mountain that overlooks Stressa, I found a large Black Prince. His castle was a spacious bar, and he chose his company from the patrons at the bar. Within moments of my arrival, his head was in my lap. Once formal introductions had been completed, he entwined himself around my legs for the remainder of my stay.

Now those with a knowledge of my visual problems and with the sentiments of the last few paragraphs may conclude that I have a seeing-eye dog or have at least a strong affection for canines. Actually, I'm somewhat afraid of dogs and have never owned one. When my friends and acquaintances urge me to get a seeing-eye dog, I tell them I'm waiting for a trained chimpanzee. I'll call him Dr. Muggs, dress him in a vest and sporting cap, and give him a tobacco-less pipe to suck on. Perched on a stool in my office, he'll be a corroborating colleague who'll agree or disagree with me based on prearranged cues. Oh, there may be a dog some day, but not yet.

One of the feelings blocking my desire for a dog is that I can't stand wasting someone's time. If I owned a dog, he would have to spend incredible amounts of time with me just hanging around. When I was at work listening to some material, the dog would be at my feet—waiting. When I taught a class, he'd be in the corner—waiting. When I went to church or to a restaurant, he'd be waiting. Even if he could stand it, it would drive me crazy!

Nonetheless, there exists one factor in the disability world that might compel me to replace my cane with a pooch—crowd appeal. As in all social groups, the disabled too have ranks and pecking order. A wheelchair receives more deference than a pair of crutches; a dog completely overshadows the stick. In short <u>canus</u> conquers cane.

Now I never thought much about this until I boarded a plane a few years ago with a woman who had a seeing-eye dog. I usually got pretty good attention when I boarded with my cane. People would ask if they could assist me, would move quickly out of my way, and in general would show some concern about me. However, when the lady with the dog entered the scene, I became more than invisible—I was non-existent. I felt like the first coed at a frat party when six of the most gorgeous cheerleaders had arrived. The dog has great public power indeed.

So, maybe someday I'll join the world of dog owners. Yet, from my experience with Rex I know that we do not own dogs; we serve them. Names like <u>Rex</u>, <u>Duke</u>, and <u>Caesar</u> are not just cute; they reflect reality.

CHAPTER 4

▼

DIABLO EX MACHINA

I stood on the corner with Athena in the heart of the city dedicated to her for millennia. Tears from her eyes bathed my left elbow as around us a cacophonous chaos raged. Like a swarm of mechanized mosquitos, motorbikes whined in an incredible array of annoying pitches. Motorcycles blasphemously matched the thunder of Zeus as they rumbled violently, more in place than in movement. Cars trumpeted their frustration with unending wails of blasting horns. If one needed a soundtrack for the horrors of hell, this was it. Athena couldn't bear how her citizens had failed her, how they had made her city an aural hell.

Even her temple, the Parthenon, has been violated. According to scientists, it is the pollution of the internal combustion engine that is currently the major threat to the wonderful monuments of the Acropolis. I could say nothing to comfort Athena, for how does one explain the madness of the machines—the costs, the alienation, the environmental devastation?

In some Greek drama a god will descend from the upper stage at the end of a play to save the day and put things right. In Latin this device is known as deus ex machina because the god is lowered in a large basket.

Ironically, the Italian word for car is machina. Certainly for Athena and others, the car and its related internal combustion machines do not offer salvation. Rather, they bring us the hell that is Athens, Palermo, Rome, London, Los Angeles, and New York. Internal combustion engines are diablo ex machina.

Yet, of course, we need them. If we live out in the country and away from possibilities of mass transit, personal motorized vehicles are indeed necessary to enjoy the benefits of modern mobility. However, two million vehicles for four million residents of Athens are just too much. Ironically, it was the Greeks who in the past trumpeted the wisdom of the golden mean—moderation in all things. This applies to vehicles as well.

Happily, the Greeks are taking some action and should have a subway system in place in time for the 2004 Olympics. Whether this addition to its public transportation network will change the traffic maelstrom in Athens remains to be seen. London and New York have excellent public transportation, but King Car refuses to abdicate. It seems as soon as drivers see the traffic jams decreasing because of public transportation, they assume that this easier access is made possible for them. This self-centered pride is, of course, diabolical.

As Nancy and I walked the sidewalks of Athens, we got a chance to see the self-centered diabolical first-hand. Although we were on the sidewalk, we had to be very, very careful—particularly at intersections. Motorcycles and motorbikes would literally cut corners and cruise across the sidewalk! Travel on other pedestrian paths was equally rife with peril. As Nancy and I were traversing one of these pedestrian walkways, I suddenly heard Nancy cry out. Alarmed, I asked her what had happened. She informed me that a van that had come up behind us had struck her with its mirror. Despite Nancy's scream, the van had continued on. Fortunately, although Nancy was shaken, she was not hurt.

The tragedy of transportation continues on in most of the major cities of the world, and it seems that even with the involvement of a goddess like Athena a happy ending may not be found. Yet, hope does spring eternal and perhaps even now Zeus is weaving a basket that will carry a solution to dry his daughters' tears and ease our car cares.

CHAPTER 5

▼

PSYCHE AND THE MOTORBIKE

Athena took her leave and sought momentary refuge at Olympus; I took public transportation to Rafina, a small port where Nancy and I had a campsite. With the sea breeze refreshing my body and a glass of wine soothing my soul, I pondered the psychology of incredibly annoying personal modes of transportation—the motorbike, the motorcycle, the snowmobile, the jet ski, the ultra light. Are the users of these vehicles unconscious of the noise they make? Do they, in fact, cherish the noise? I think it's the latter.

Back in the days of hierarchy rather than individualism, members of the royalty and aristocracy would announce their coming with a specific trumpet call, one which identified a specific nobleman. Today, in a world of six billion people, individuals want to claim they are special. People want to say, "Here I am!" One can do this through vocational accomplishment, artistic achievement, or public service. However, these paths take work and talent. Being noisy takes neither talent nor work.

In addition to gaining attention, the noisemaker also gets to exert power over many others. In most cases this perverse power is the only power these individuals will have.

I thought of several cases that demonstrated the truth of this observation so very clearly. Nancy and I had gone to Delphi to see the shrine of the Oracle—the Sibyl. The region was sacred and magical to the ancients; it remains so today. We were camped on an escarpment several thousand feet above the sea. Mountains extended to our left, and a small village lay several hundred feet beneath us. It was about six in the evening, and the campground was more than half full, yet, there was almost no noise—no radios and precious little conversation. It was as if all the campers sensed the natural beauty and mystical vibrations of this site. How outraged I became when a single individual on an ultra light broke the silence with the soul-splitting, aural atrocity of an internal combustion engine. Flying above and beyond us for a half hour, he destroyed a special experience for thousands of people. Perhaps harshly, but perhaps not, I wished that the Daedalus/Icarus legend could be played out in the present. What right did this person have to be here so arrogantly, so insensitively, so stupidly?

Of course, similar acts occur all the time. On Mykonos, Nancy and I were enjoying a peaceful moment in a lovely cove when someone climbed aboard a jet ski and ground our peaceful into shattered shards. The rider had to be aware of the noise. My only conclusion is that the childish need of "look at me, Mommy" and the urge to exercise power over others destroy every sense of consideration and sensitivity to others.

However, we must not forget the devils who provide these engines of the immature for profit. As transportation all of these vehicles could be made to perform much more quietly and just as safely. Why aren't they? The answer is that an installation of sound insulation would increase the cost of the vehicle. Ah, yes, it would also lower the shout of "look at me!" to the level of polite conversation. But the inventors and manufacturers are not worried about others. If the gods can provide justice, they will assign the inventors of the snowmobile and jet ski to an eternity of root canals.

The gods do assign punishment to the users of noise vehicles although it is questionable whether the punishment is sufficient and free of unintended consequences. What the gods inflict upon the noise riders goes by the name of sociocusis. This process occurs as hearing is damaged by excessive noise in one's surroundings. A musician in a heavy metal band or a motorcyclist on a high decibel bike will lose much of his hearing ability by the time he is in his mid-forties. For those open to the conversation and ideas of others, this would be a tragic condition. It's less tragic if one is not so open.

With regard to unintended consequences of the gods' punishment, the excessively loud restaurant patron comes to mind. Suffering from diminished hearing through sociocusis, this middle-aged person talks as if he is giving a speech to the entire restaurant. Since the speaker cannot hear himself well, he has no idea how loud his volume really is. As a result a relaxing, romantic, and intimate dining experience becomes "Kids Eat Free" day at McDonald's. Since motorcycles and jet skis, and ultra-lights cost money, these deaf declaimers can be found in a wide range of restaurants, including upscale bistros.

Defenders of the noise machines might claim that noise is a safety element. If this were so, we should equip bicyclists with amplified motorcycle tapes and cross-country skiers and canoeists with boom boxes. Modern cars have significant sound insulation to keep out road noise. In addition, most have high-output stereos that mask outside noises. When the Dopler effect with regard to moving noises is added to the equation, the result is that loud motor noise does not help in the exact locating of the noisy vehicle. The fact that cars are often oblivious to the specially designed wails of emergency vehicles should be ample proof of this.

No, sometimes it just comes down to ignorance and inconsideration. Like Odysseus' men who opened Aeolus' bag of wind and later ate the forbidden cattle of Helios, some folks just don't get it. Unfortunately, like the long-suffering Odysseus, we must share in the misery produced by others. Because the bag of wind was opened, Odysseus and his men were blown many leagues away from home, just when they could see the smoke rising from the cooking fires in their homes. Likewise, we suffer like Odysseus when his ship was wrecked after his men committed sacrilege by eating the cattle of the sun god despite being forbidden to do so. Our wayward travelers are equally inconsiderate as they ruthlessly violate our peace and quiet. They are punished for their transgression, but we all lose the peace that rightfully should be ours.

Chapter 6

▼

Of Mycenae and Men

Travel to archaeological sites does not usually attract a lot of blind people. The sites often involve a climb over very uneven stairs and very rough ground. When a blind person gets to the site, what will he see? In my case I have retained enough sight to see shadows and silhouettes, and, if the light is just right, the view of bright columns against a dark hillside.

But there are other senses beyond sight. As Nancy and I move, I feel the topography beneath my feet. I'm able to tune out the babbling of tourists and hear the natural sounds that are part of the place. The wind hums the hymn it has sounded for millennia, and like the grating roar of the seashore that took Matthew Arnold back to the Aegean in "Dover Beach," I am transported to a former time—a time much slower, and for that reason, perhaps more meaningful than our frenetic present. Then there are the smells of sea and forest that complete my sense of place. Is my experience as full as that of a sighted person? Perhaps not, but it will serve.

On the sacred island of Delos, for example, I was able to traverse the flat distances of this small island and to feel under my feet the ruined remains of the homes and shops once inhabited by 30,000 people from all over the Mediterranean. I was able to see the hill of some 300 feet that gives some topographical variety to this birthplace of Apollo and Artemis, the one-time treasury of the Delian League.

Of all the sites on our agenda, the one that held particular interest for me was Agamemnon's Palace at Mycenae. As I read Aeschylus' play, Agamemnon, in which the treacherous Clytemnestra murders her heroic husband in his bath, I couldn't get the opening scenes out of my mind. The setting is the terrace of the palace. Clearly there is a view of the sea—the route that all the victorious Greeks would use to return from Troy. Perhaps inspired by Athena, my imagination had cut through the mists of the unknown and developed a very strong image of what this terrace and its view were like. I had to experience this for myself. The problem was that the path to the remains of the palace would be the hardest to climb of all the dozens of sites we visited. Indeed, the "path" was a nightmare. The 200 foot climb starts with what is called "the great ramp." It is a misnomer. It is narrow, extremely slippery, and about twenty-five feet long. Then the fun begins. The path is actually a channel of boulders, rocks, and debris. I felt that over the centuries all the soil between this material had eroded away. Some of the rocks were firm; some were loose. All were on an incline; all were unforgiving. Where could I step? Where could I put my cane? How could I keep my balance? The goddess Athena joined with Nancy's spirit to give her a patience and precision unknown to mortals. Painstakingly and perceptively, she analyzed each square inch of terrain and then told me where and in what order each of my three limbs—left leg, right leg, cane—should be placed. It was tedious work, but any mistake would lead to a bad bruise, a sprained ankle, a fracture, or worse. Sighted people around us fell; others did not make the climb. I had to get to the palace!

The sun beat upon us. The heat and tension drenched my shirt. Halfway up, my courage faltered for a second; I was frightened. But going down was more dangerous than going up—so I climbed. After a half hour and with arms trembling, I made the terrace. The palace was essentially gone, but the floor remained, and what I could see of the view was a miracle. It was exactly as I had imagined it—the sea perspective, the noble hills—everything! No wonder Athena wanted me to be here.

Of course, the problem now was to get down. Gravity would now become a treacherous accelerator, not a force inhibitor. Unlike American parks there were no rangers to call for help, no golf cart to take one down the back side of the mountain. I stalled as long as I could; then we began to descend. Nancy informed me early on that I could not leave the path; the drop-off on either side would lead to severe injury. I moved slowly, not anticipating the end, but concentrating on the precise movement and placement of each limb. I put my left foot on a stone the size of a basketball. It seemed firm; then it moved! For a brief second I was gravity's victim. Adrenaline exploded. My weight shifted to my cane. The graphite bent, but the cane was fixed and firm. I could continue.

The path was dangerous; the path was narrow. Ironically, the path was also crowded. Because there was a destination and a route to it, people assumed it was safe. It wasn't. People were routinely slipping and losing their balance. The crowding limited stepping options, and the pressure to speed up made mistakes inevitable. About one-third down, the side drop-off was gradual, and Nancy took us off the path. Slowly we climbed down the surface of the hill. When we looked back we were astonished to see a few other tourists following us! Had they imagined me to be some blind Tiresias, or had they come to the conclusion that the route of a blind man must be easier? It wasn't. Eventually all options petered out, and we were forced back to the path. Fortunately, the steepest part was done, and with a patience nurtured by apprehension, we reached the bottom.

This visit to Agamemnon's palace was the hardest experience I had had as a blind person; it was also one of the most rewarding. I had been afraid; I had been courageous; I had been lucky. Most of all, I had put my trust in Nancy, who with a clearly superhuman effort, enabled me to complete this journey I so longed to take.

The palace at Mycenae was certainly the most arduous destination Nancy and I faced in our travels. I had heard that the Acropolis was difficult, but I found this to be an overstatement. One has a strenuous climb to this high city, but the stairs are reasonably even and predictable for a blind person, and the path is generally smooth and without rubble and debris. A much more strenuous journey is the trek to the top of Delphi to stand at the athletic stadium. On the way one passes treasure houses, the seat of the Oracle, Apollo's temple, and the theater. The natural setting is fabulous, but the steps are unevenly made and spaced. Some are but an inch or so high; others rise as high as fifteen inches or so. Furthermore, the actual vertical ascent seemed higher than that to the Acropolis. However, like the palace at Mycenae, both sites more than repay whatever physical exertion they require.

Often what makes site visitation for the unsighted more difficult than it need be is the behavior of the sighted. Now, I carry the official white cane as a visual aid for both myself and those who see me. I tap the stairs with it as I hold Nancy's elbow. I can't imagine what more I can do. Some people seem to catch on. Others are like zombies from Night of the Living Dead. They walk around in random directions with their mouths wide open as flies do touch and go landings on their tongues. Groups like to stop at narrow landings to block any and all passage. Our passage through the Delphi site was more difficult because of the human factor than for any topographical reason.

Speaking of groups, I must say that nothing ruins a ruin for me more than the arrival of the dreaded tour buses with their instant congestion and confusion. Now I know they have their place, but they certainly have their costs as well. Some of the blame has to go to their guides. At Siracusa several buses arrived at the same time and just about stopped any movement at the site. The guides brought several hundred people to wait at the ticket area while the guides went about obtaining entrance tickets for the members of their groups. Unfortunately, the junction of main paths is relatively near the ticket booth. The crowds overflowed, and no one could move. It was awful.

In addition, there's something that happens psychologically on a tour bus that makes its members different from other tourists. First, the bus ride quickly becomes the main psychological tether. Site visits become interruptions to the ride. Secondly, since the group members know a guide will lecture on the site at the site, many do little or no preparation for what they are about to see. As a result, they're not in the proper frame of mind when they get off the bus. Social conversations started on the bus replace historical reflection and creative imagining. Of course, neither speculation nor imagining are easy to achieve as guides at a site jabber to their groups in Italian, Japanese, German, French, English, and Greek—all at the same time. I often imagined I was at the Tower of Babel rather than a Greek temple of the sixth century, B. C.

Yet, at one level the cacophony of languages brought a clear meaning. These sites were of interest not just to one culture or one set of language users. They were of interest to all humanity. The story of the Ancient Greeks and Romans was not only about those peoples of the past but somehow also about us in the present. As we seek to find out who they were as people, we find out something about ourselves as humans.

One additional point was not lost upon me as I mused about the usefulness and desirability of bus tours. Certainly the major considerations for those in the bus tour were comfort, convenience, and certainty. The price was the distraction and crowding of the group and a certain disconnectedness from the process of travel. Without the connection to the process the sites might seem somehow artificial in much the same way that scenes in a house of horrors ride in an amusement park seem contrived as we come upon them in our vehicle.

I was certainly part of the process as Nancy and I discussed all the logistics of our upcoming days of travel. To be frank, I must say that sometimes the lack of certainty produced stress. At other times the sheer effort of travel—finding sites, finding restaurants, finding overnight accommodations—finding, finding, finding—caused fatigue and anxiety. Yet, for me there was a great deal of comfort, convenience and certitude. Nancy was incredibly thorough in her research. It had begun months before we left and continued throughout each day of our trip. I had traveled much with her and trusted her knowledge of our options without question. She trusted my decision-making and financial sense. Yet, when all was said and done, she was the one who read, drove, and toiled. I had the best of it all—independent travel with the ease of a good tour. Nancy bore the burden. For this I will be eternally grateful.

CHAPTER 7

▼

HARPIES IN MINIATURE

When I was a child, our family sought relief from the hot and humid summers in Bayonne, New Jersey, by visiting the summer home of my Aunt Adele and Uncle Stanley in Waretown, New Jersey, adjacent to Bornegat Bay. It was the late 1950s, and the development that is so prominent now was just beginning then. In fact there was a frontier flavor to the place. The few houses that included Adele's were surrounded by pine trees, and the property across the road was completely forested.

This frontier liberated my brothers, sister, and me. Free from the asphalt asphyxiation of Bayonne, we followed my cousin Judy to pick wild blueberries, climb trees, and explore unknown paths. On days of longer hikes we walked to the lagoon fed by the bay and saw Uncle Stanley's boat, The Chief. Although it was only a sixteen-foot rowboat with a small motor and was usually partially submerged, the Chief was an object of deep admiration for us. It represented the possibility of boat rides, crabbing, and maybe even fishing! It opened up the seas of the world.

In the meantime as we waited for possibility to become actuality, there was Aunt Adele and her house to enjoy. Adele possessed a fun-loving spirit and spent most of the day not wearing any shoes. A marginal cook, she often declared that her burned hot dogs and hamburgers were "charcoal brown." The house shared her easy-going personality. For example, there was a roofless wooden shower outside the house. This afforded me my first opportunity to be naked in the outdoors, and it felt quite racy. Nearly all of the meals were served in a large, screened porch. For a child of eleven it was nearly heaven. But it was not heaven, for there was one hellish element that polluted this paradise and curtailed happiness—the mosquito.

Now, as a resident of Hudson County in the 50's, I was familiar with the mosquito as a health danger and a pest that government officials needed to control. The Bayonne Times frequently had front-page articles describing the county's mosquito problems. However the city mosquitos were nothing compared to their country cousins. As the sun set in Waretown, the mosquitos exploded from their hiding places in swarms. We were advised not to leave the house, and only to leave if we were bathed in 6-12, the flagship repellant of the day.

The developers and officials of the Waretown region were not unaware of the threat posed by the mosquito, not only to health but to the future growth of the area, so they mounted a very vigorous mosquito extermination campaign. Each evening a jeep equipped with an insecticide fogger would drive through the area. Huge clouds of insecticide would roll over everything and everybody. Blueberries, bikes, and unattended hot dogs would all disappear behind this veil of chemical death. The cloud would seep into Adele's screened porch as we ate. The cloud smelled a bit, but it was good—it meant death to the enemies of paradise.

With this background, therefore, I was somewhat intrigued by movies filmed in Europe that I saw in subsequent years. The houses had no screens! This could only mean that there were no mosquitos. In fact, there mustn't be flying insects of any kind, for a basic axiom of life states that screens were necessary to deter flying insects—and the absence of screens could only occur without such insects. It seemed like a logical and true theorem. It was false, as I learned one night in the Bois de Bologne, a large park in Paris that contains a campground. It was 1973, and Nancy and I were camping in a stripped Ford van we had rented from a Dutch firm. Sleeping on a comfortable air mattress, I was suddenly awakened by those wicked whines from hell that fill one's ears in the wee hours of the morning. All the windows of the van were closed, but somehow—perhaps through unclosable vents—those harpies in miniature had come to terrorize me. I swatted and sighed, sighed and swatted. I had many kills—but I had no sleep. From this point on we abandoned the comfort of the truck for the harpy-proof crampness of our pup tent. Bare windows, I sadly learned, did not equate with freedom from mosquitos.

Sadly, history repeats, and those who fail to learn from history are doomed to repeat its mistakes. I suffer from such a historical learning disability—at least to some degree. Nancy and I had been in Greece in 2001 for about ten days. We had tented for two days, gotten a room, and rented an apartment for a week. In that time I had encountered perhaps three mosquitos. They weren't annoyances; they were more like relics or curiosities. Of course it stood to reason that Greece would have few mosquitos—at least to me.

Mosquitos breed in standing water and hide among leafy vegetation. Greece had neither. It was rocky and arid. As Nancy and I settled into the bungalow we had rented at a Rafina campground, my mind was free of thoughts of insects. Greece's May winds were howling at about 45 mph from the Bay of Rafina. Our hut rattled and shook; the plywood walls creaking against the children of Aeolus, god of the winds. As the night wore on, I rolled incessantly in my sagging cot. Just as I would enter REM sleep, I would awaken as a new blast from the bay seemed to rip the roof shingles from our little hut. When Aurora filled the dawn with her light, I was awake to greet her. I was exhausted but unbitten.

The next day Aeolus had placed all his winds in his magical bag. I welcomed the approach of night and softly sagged into slumber. But the harpies wouldn't have it so. Within minutes of my first doze there was one mosquito in my left ear. I swatted at it and missed. Simultaneously, another penetrated my right ear. A third perched on my eyebrow. I was all hands and arms. I rained blows on the harpies, hit a few, but mostly pummeled myself fruitlessly. Getting sleep became secondary to avoiding bites. As dawn signaled the cessation of hostilities and the end of the night's ordeal, I was tired, cranky, nauseous, and bespeckled over my head and arms with the mounded monuments of the harpies' triumph. I had been defeated.

Nancy had hardly been touched during my night of torment. The harpies are particular about whom they victimize. Nonetheless, she graciously joined my efforts to prepare for the next evening's hostilities. Where had our defenses been weak? How had they gotten in? We hadn't planned on being attacked, so we hadn't planned our defenses. As she glanced over the hut, Nancy assured me that there was only one flaw in our defensive perimeter—our very door itself! The door, it seems, was too small to fill its space. At some places it left an opening of at least three-quarters of an inch. At other places, the gap narrowed. Few, however, were the areas where the door actually filled its frame. It appeared upon close examination to have been made and installed by the worst vocational crafts student in history. A "D" grade for this door would have been a gift.

Having identified the problem, we now looked for a solution. The breach could not be effectively filled by towels. The gap was often too small, and the towels would fall from their own weight. Athena did not wish her son to be tormented this night, and so she whispered the simplest of solutions into my waiting mind. I then instructed Nancy to use long strips of toilet paper to cover the gaps and to affix them to the frame with scotch tape. Of no strength to us but posing an impenetrable barrier to the mosquitos, the toilet paper worked just fine. I slept in the bosom of Athena and awoke with the freshness of a god. The only negative was the somewhat tawdry impression our doorway toilet paper streamers might have made on some of the French campers nearby. C'est la vie! The harpies had been defeated, but they were not disheartened. Their obsession with me went back decades. A few squares of toilet paper would not be sufficient to eliminate their hatred.

The next encounter came but a few days later. We were staying in one of Mina's studios on the island of Mykonos. It was a clean dwelling, inexpensively priced, with a nice couple running it. Again, there were no screens; again there were mosquitos. This time Athena took the form of a housemaid. When we mentioned the mosquitos, she produced what I thought was a night light and plugged it into the wall outlet. Hephestus himself never made weapons so deadly. Essentially, a miniature bug zapper, this device uses an aromatic scent—much like my own bodily fragrance I would think—that draws the mosquitos to it. Then, the same voltage that can create worlds of pictures on the TV screen ends the world of the mosquito in an instantaneous, obliterating flash. Once we became armed, the harpies kept their distance.

But I am slow to learn. At the beach's edge on the Gargano Promontory in Italy, Nancy and I secured another bungalow. This was no hut. It had two bedrooms, toilet and shower, and a large cement room with sink and appliances that opened to the sea. This large room had an entrance but no door, and an opening but no window. The bedroom area did have a door that closed. Here I assumed I was safe. We had screens in our bedroom for inner protection. We had an outer room that lacked not only screens but windows themselves. If there were mosquitos, nobody would build a room like that. Even if there were mosquitos, we were protected; our bedroom had screens.

Armed with this certainty Nancy and I settled in each other's arms. Like that of Odysseus and Penelope, our bed offered comfort, security, and peace. This peace was shortly shattered by the howls of numerous harpies. Again, I slapped, punched, and swatted; I hit myself so many times I began to feel like a club fighter. Then the goddess, the glorious Athena, saw my plight and took pity on me. Taking the form of Nancy, she brandished a rolled-up magazine as her weapon. She turned on the overhead light and danced upon the bed covers. Her blows to the mosquitos on the ceiling cracked like thunder. Quickly, inevitably, the mosquitoes gave up their life blood. The goddess ended the mean work of the harpies upon me just as she had done for Orestes, son of tragic Agamemnon and treacherous Clytemnestra. Then turning out the light, she restored Nancy to me, and we slept the soundest of sleeps.

The next day we purchased our own mosquito zapper—top of the line, good for forty-five nights. Nancy also discovered scores of harpies hiding in the closet. Waiting there smelling my body like turkey cooking on Thanksgiving morning, they would be impatient to attack. Fortunately, the zapper took on all comers, and Nancy and I vowed to install it whenever a room would have an appropriate outlet. I had been a victim of the harpies for fifty years. At last, under the protection of Athena, I was free of their sting.

CHAPTER 8

▼

CHARON'S FERRY TALES

Our age moves by land and air. Cars and planes are our vehicles of choice. Fast and convenient, they take us quickly where we need to go. Ships, on the other hand, are a novelty for most of us. Part of the fun of a boat ride or a cruise is that it is unusual. For the ancients, a boat was a speedy and safe way to travel. Sure, there were pirates, but there were far fewer pirates at sea than brigands and desperadoes on land. In addition three or four knots (about four miles per hour) of speed could often be maintained on sea for extended periods, whereas 10-15 miles of travel per day would be the most that could be expected on land, even in the best of circumstances. In this ancient world, sea travel was comparatively speedy.

Oddly enough, safety and relative speed still exist in the Mediterranean. For example, the ferry from Genoa to Palermo is a twenty-four hour voyage. The same trip by car would easily consume two days and also result in an exhausted driver and passengers. Safety and convenience also enter into the trip from Brindisi in Italy to Patras in Greece. The trip by land would take one through the Balkans—not a playground for holiday makers. Thus, it is not surprising that maps of the Mediterranean are filled with the dotted lines of ferry routes that offer safe point-to-point travel at a reasonable cost.

Nancy and I took the Genoa to Palermo ferry when Nancy looked at the mileage chart and saw how many kilometers of high-speed terror she would have to endure to get us from Genoa to Sicily. I should also mention that Americans have a rather limited notion of what a ferry is. Our childhood experience tells us that a ferry is a small, flat boat with an open deck that can accommodate about six cars. In reality, the European ferries are much, much larger. The SS. Excellent, for example, which took us from Genoa to Palermo, is about the size of a World War II battleship. It is over 600 feet long and displaces nearly 40,000 tons. Painted white, it could easily be identified as a cruise ship. Indeed, with several restaurants, numerous cabins, a show room, piano bar, and discotheque, this ship offered both comfort and entertainment.

Speaking of comfort, I did not hesitate to book a cabin for our overnight passage. Now a cabin with full bath is the most expensive way to travel on a ferry, and costs about an additional $100, the price of a decent hotel room. Less expensive is a reservation for an airplane-type seat in a sleeping lounge. However, since I can rarely sleep on an airplane, I found the concept only moronic. The cheapest accommodation is mere passage. Here the passenger gets no reserved sleeping place and finds a place on deck to bed down in a sleeping bag on a mat. This, of course, is the sleeping bag and mat that the passenger has carried on board. The idea sounds romantic at 10 PM if one is about twenty years old. At 6 AM, however, after a night on pitching steel, everyone on deck, no matter the age, looks and feels like seventy.

By the way, there are no harder surfaces than those of ships. This is particularly demanding for the blind. Any fall or error will bring one into contact with the hardest of surfaces. In addition, stairs are often steep, especially leading from the parking areas in the hold. Furthermore, ship construction calls for raised crossbeams along the floor— something very different from construction on land.

Another thing different about ships that non-seamen do not realize is that ships swim. That is, they don't just move through water as a fixed object; rather they move their entire bodies in twisting and struggling ways as they attempt to ply the waves. Great physical forces push and pull at the ship at the bow and the sides. Swells lift and drop the hull as waves push in a direction often perpendicular to forward movement. Of course, while all of this is going on, the ship's engines drive a great propeller that insistently pushes thousands of tons of water from the path of the ship. Naturally, there is some vibration. In addition, there is a twisting and a pulling at every rivet and joint of the ship in much the same way that there is a twisting and pulling at every joint in the body of a swimmer. The swimmer survives the play of these forces because he has strengthened his muscles through training and maximized his flexibility through stretching exercises. Ships have to follow a similar regimen. Some of the hastily build merchant ships of World War II actually broke in half in the Atlantic because they did not have sufficient strength and flexibility to deal with the heavy seas of the North Atlantic. The SS. Excellent certainly had strength, but its flexibility was short of perfection. Its builders had built the tolerances too close in the construction of the cabins and not allowed sufficient space for the ship's movement. As a result, the ends of the modern composite materials that formed the cabin and its appointments creaked and chafed against each other. The interior designer did not realize that SS. Excellent was a swimmer. The SS. Maria G of the Medlink fleet, on the other hand, is a marvelous example of flexibility. Much older than SS. Excellent, it presented almost no creaking as we steamed across the Adriatic.

Another thing about the big ferries is that they uplift the spirit. Experiencing the automobile anarchy of urban Athens or the insane crush of an Alitalia boarding process, one might lose hope in the future of humanity. For many years I found two human endeavors that caused me optimism. The first was opera. How incredible it is that any opera is ever performed! Scores of singers must coordinate with scores of instrumentalists and be backed up by scores of production people. It is live, split-second, on-pitch, and beautiful. If human beings can do this, they can do anything. The second human activity that underscores hope is the way people get off ski lifts without killing themselves. When I recall my skiing days, I remember that getting off the chair lift was always the most challenging part of the run. Yet, ordinary people do it every day in a rather routine way. Poles, ski tips, uncoordinated amateurs, and a moving piece of technology all come together on a slippery surface without disaster. It gives me hope.

The loading and unloading of motor vehicles on the ferry provides equal inspiration. It amazes me how people can drive their $20,000 cars up and down narrow ramps into the dark holds of ships and park within a few inches of the unforgiving metal hull. These drivers have been given no instruction, nor do they know exactly where they are going. The worst is to be first in line. I recall my admiration for Nancy as she drove our $24,000 car up a narrow ramp with no guard rails to get on the ferry Aphrodite for our journey from Brindisi to Patras. Actually, Nancy was experiencing a sense of relief at the time, for the circus caravan with wild animals that she thought would be boarding with us was instead boarding the ferry at the next berth. To be at sea with tigers on the loose or snakes under sail was not the European adventure she longed for.

Even more impressive than the loading of personal vehicles is what happens with trucks. Not only do tractor-trailers use the same narrow ramps, they also have to back on in many instances. Many of the ferries have just one exit. To expedite debarkation, the back-up positioning is done at the front end of the trip. How marvelous it is to witness the skill of the drivers as they maneuver their big rigs amidst the cries and signal choreography of those guiding them to their parking slots. If people can do this day after day without mishap, what promise it holds for what is possible!

While the big ferries inspire us with a sense of the possible, the smaller high-speed ferries impress us with their speed and agility. As

Nancy and I toyed with the idea of visiting a few Greek islands, we consulted several travel books on the topic. In general these guides spoke of crowding and the difficulty of obtaining hotel accommodations—even in May. They also created a picture of the ferry situation as somewhat haphazard. Our experience was different on both counts. We got a clean accommodation with bath, refrigerator, and TV for about $22 a night at Mina's Studios. We took three high-speed catamarans and got to our destination on time. However, there were some interesting wrinkles.

The Greeks, as a people, live in and for the moment. As a result they are not inclined to make reservations or advanced bookings. Nancy and I went to book passage on a Flying Dolphin catamaran to Mykonos on a Wednesday afternoon. We felt somewhat guilty about the fact that we wanted tickets for the next day. The clerk informed us that a general strike had just been called for Thursday and no boats would be sailing. We booked tickets for Friday. The catamaran had an airplane-like interior. The cabin was similar to a 747 and had about 400 numbered seats. As far as I could determine, Nancy and I were among the first 40 to make reservations for a Friday afternoon sailing, yet all 400 seats were filled. This last-minute faith in accommodation availability was repeated over and over again in our travels. Tourists were always early and at the head of the line, but just a few moments before departure, the Greeks would come—hopeful and happy.

While the cabins of catamarans looked like those of airplanes, there was one very obvious difference—there was no storage space for luggage of any kind in the cabin. In fact luggage storage seems to have been an afterthought in the design of these vessels. As Nancy and I boarded, a crewman took our large backpack and placed it on deck with whatever other bags were given to him. This area filled quickly, and there were no luggage tags. At stops, passengers plowed through the pile and grabbed their bags. Limited in space and security, this "system" motivated many people to keep their bags with them. As a result, the aisles were filled with baggage. Often there was no path. As I headed toward the restroom, I often encountered a baggage blockade. However, once a passenger saw I needed to get through, he would pick up his bags, open the passage, and then fill it in behind me as I passed. Most Americans, I think, would find the on-deck luggage setup and the aisle storage method to be intolerable or unacceptable. Indeed, I found myself muttering about the inefficiency and lack of security of it all. However, a few moments reflection as I sipped a Mythos beer brought other, more positive views. The on-deck luggage system was, in fact, a statement of trust. People would be clever enough to find their own bags and honest enough to leave the bags of others alone. More than that, the idea lingered that the bag, the material possession, was not that important after all. People and experience were primary; bags were accessories. This is something I will always think about as I witness an irate passenger demean and belittle an airline employee over a bagful of mostly used clothes.

The in-aisle baggage storage also said something positive. I viewed the situation as an intolerable inconvenience because I was thinking as an isolated individual and was impatient. When I saw myself as part of the ship's community, I recalled how people gladly moved the luggage to make way for me if I couldn't get through. We were literally all in the same boat. As such we needed to have patience and to respect a sense of community.

This sense of community surfaced strongly on other occasions. On Mykonos there are converted fishing boats that ferry passengers from one beach to another. Two of the more famous beaches on the island are Paradise Beach and Super Paradise Beach. The first is known for its music; the latter for its lack of a dress code—or should I say, its lack of dress. Naturally we had to experience both, so we sought out the beach taxi. Boarding at the beach near our room was no problem. There was a dock, and numerous hands and arms helped me into the seating area when the passengers saw my cane. At the Paradise beaches, however, there was no dock. The bow of the boat beached itself in about a foot of water, and that was it. There had been no warning about this when we boarded—but why should there have been? Passengers simply removed their shoes, scurried along the deck, and descended a bow ladder into the water. I, of course, presented a problem. The placement of feet around ropes and fittings demanded sight as did the descent down the narrow and steep ladder. How amazing it was that people immediately saw the problem and the need to help. A retired civil engineer from Australia took over for Nancy. Was he Athena in disguise? He was taller than I was, and his muscular arms assured me that I could disembark without fear of injury. In the boarding process on the return trip, the choreography of assistance played itself out just as beautifully. One passenger took my cane, and a young man in great physical condition nearly hoisted me upon the bow and out of the water. We didn't even have to ask for help. It was given freely and immediately.

Before the trip I had worried about our trips by sea—I imagined chaos, crowding, and a lack of dependability. What I found was comfort, a sense of community, and a welcome break from the incarceration of the automobile.

However, just as a trip with Charon, the ferryman over the river Styx, was not without its negatives—one was, after all, going to Hades—so also did my sea-going travels prompt some concerns. First, for me, was the question of seasickness. Now somewhere in the bowels of American social consciousness I know it is unmanly to be sea sick, but it's not a matter of psychology but of physiology. In addition, from what I've read even experienced inter-ocean sailors get green in the gills at the start of a trip or in very heavy seas. Thus, my admissions here should not be cause of undue shame. Yes, I do get seasick-Nancy does not. Sometimes I begin to feel queasy even while we're still at the dock. My solution to the problem is Dramamine. If I follow the directions, I don't have any trouble although I've found the drowsy kind impacts me like a three-hour lecture on municipal government models in a public administration course. I never took any chances here. Even light swells can bring on the symptoms, and a forty minute passage can seem like forty years once Poseidon has gotten someone in his sickly grip.

Another concern I had about the ferries was getting to them on time but not leaving too much time to kill. Here, again Athena and Nancy joined forces to keep the waiting time reasonable although in our longer ferry journeys from Genoa to Palermo, and Brindisi to Patros, the departure time was not train-like. In fact, one of the benefits of a cabin was that it always seemed more beneficial for me to wait for departure while I was reclining on a bed with my head on a clean pillow.

Another concern was the sheer terror of the car-loading process on the ferries. The key problem in this process was a conflict of objectives. Nancy and I just wanted to get our car on the boat. The loaders wanted us to use as little space as possible so they would have as much room as possible. As it was their boat, they eventually won. They yelled, waved, gesticulated, and performed all sorts of antics to get Nancy to put our new car within an inch of permanently scratching steel. We both waited for the sound of that sorrowful scratching screech, but thanks to the gods and Nancy's depth perception, it never occurred.

Yet, in spite of our successful parking experiences, we were always fearful during ferry parking. One day was particularly irritating. We were taking a small ferry outside of Patros for a journey of less than two hours. The ferry was small and could accommodate about twenty-four cars on deck. Since it was mid-week in May, only five cars had lined up on the dock for the crossing. However, when boarding began, the crew acted as if twenty-five cars were waiting. They crowded the six cars that eventually boarded into a tiny corner of the port side. Of course, our car had the privilege of being up against the steel bulkhead. Again and again, the Greek crewman harangued Nancy to gain an additional centimeter closer to the bulkhead. After about four minutes, it was done.

As we left port, Nancy and I surveyed the deck from the passenger lounge above. The six cars were packed in below us, and the nearly empty deck with the cars in the corner reminded me of a nearly consumed can of sardines. In fact, there was room enough for a soccer match to break out. Nancy exclaimed, "Just look at all that room!"

As we sipped some beer, we tried to understand the crew's point of view. Greeks are wonderfully optimistic: it's part of their national charm-we supposed the crew wanted to be ready for a sudden rush of business, and while such a rush had not occurred within the memory of any of the crewmen, it could occur. A large funeral procession of eighteen cars could arrive—perhaps—someday.

CHAPTER 9

▼

THE SINS OF HERMES

I could always trust Athena to be there when I needed her. Hermes was another matter. He, of course, served as messenger of the gods. Perhaps I was guilty of hubris, or tragic pride, in thinking that he would serve me. I, after all, am not a god—not even a minor one. But like most Americans I have been told, through years of advertising, that I certainly am close to being one. After all, how many times have I been told that I deserve certain magnificent material possessions merely because I am me. In fact, I have been told that I deserve so many things—from the finest homes, autos, and food—that I believe even the Roman emperors would envy me. Caligula, I'm sure, would be mad to possess what I deserve, and the Roman emperors were gods, weren't they? At least that's what their publicists put out. In any case, like most Americans, I had become convinced through American materialistic advertising that I was as good as Caligula—godlike and deserving of Hermes' service.

That my divine message service would not reflect perfection became clear with my association with AT&T. About a year and a half before our trip, my son spent a semester in England with a group of students from Exeter. I had been watching lots of commercials that made it seem that telephone communication was in the realm of everyday reality—20 cents a minute or so. After my first bill of $400 from MCI, my long-distance carrier at the time, I realized I was not living in reality but in sucker heaven. My son was being charged a $6.70 connection fee every time he called. Since we have an answering machine, he always got through. He'd hang up after a short message, but there was always that initial big hit. I'm sure that MCI would blame the British. I called MCI to try to get a better deal. I'm not sure I did. The bill went down by half, but then again, we were talking only half as much of the time. I'm really never sure when I'm getting a straight deal from Hermes' minions—the telecommunications companies. They sign me up at their "best" rate, and I then see an ad from them for an even better rate. When I call, the company will often change my rate, but it seems like a rip-off to me. It's like plane tickets and grocery coupons. Why can't there just be a price for something? Why do we always have to have the hustle and the special deal—and the sense we are being cheated and misled?

After this experience with my son's calls, I knew I needed to take some action. Soon after, Verizon, my local phone company, went on strike. Phone systems in the New York City area that served the handicapped and elderly were vandalized and sabotaged. I had some pretty clear ideas about who was doing such awful things, so I was ready to drop Verizon too. AT&T said they would pay me $75 to switch. I was theirs.

With my son's British phone experience behind me, I was very careful in calling AT&T about my needs for phone service from Italy, Sicily, and Greece. The calling card I was getting would allow me to call the U. S. for about 28 cents a minute with an 89 cent connection fee. There was also a $3.00 monthly charge. This seemed fine to me. I thought I was all set. About three weeks before we were to leave for Italy, I received my AT&T international calling cards. As Nancy and I examined them, we noticed that our PIN number—the element that provided security—was indelibly printed in large type on the card itself. This was insanity! Why would anyone ever want such a card? If it were lost or stolen, the unauthorized user would have the PIN number instantly in his possession. I reacted by calling AT&T. I was assured I would have new calling cards before I left. They did not arrive.

Once in Italy, we tried to call home with our cards. The operator told us they were invalid. I wanted to know why and asked for customer service. Now, one of the great mysteries of life is why places are called "customer service" when no such service is available. Clark Howard on the radio says the real phrase should be "customer disservice," and I agree with him. To give service, one needs critical-thinking skills to solve problems, knowledge of the products sold, and some latitude to make decisions. From what I've experienced over the last few years, the overwhelming majority of "customer service" reps are shut out in all three categories. AT&T was no exception. All I was able to get from the rep was that my card would not work, a fact that I already knew all too well. However, as she repeated this mantra that the card wouldn't work, I realized what probably had happened. Because Nancy and I were not going to be home for three months, we were having our mail forwarded. When our revised cards came late, they needed to be forwarded. AT&T probably has a "do not forward" policy on the cards. The cards were sent back and subsequently invalidated. I tried to communicate this scenario to the rep, but there was no mental processing of information going on. She just repeated what she had already said. After a half hour I gave up.

The next night I tried again while Nancy and my daughter, Kate, just shook their heads. This operator listened to my scenario and said the problem could be solved. She gave us slightly different card numbers, and I thought we were in business. We weren't. The next night I tried to call my sister, who was handling our bills. I was told my new card was invalid. According to the operator the only number I could call was my residence. But Nancy and I were the only residents of that residence, and we were both in Italy! There was no one there to call.

The presentation of such absurdity had no effect; our cards, I was told, were invalid.

After this event, Nancy and I buried our cards deeply in our important papers. Hopelessly romantic, we held onto them. Perhaps, someday, they would have a purpose and function effectively. For the rest of the trip we tried to make calls at coin-operated and credit-card phones, usually with exasperating results. An Italian or Greek voice would come on the phone and speak very rapidly. We would interject some English most of the time and our coins would clatter down the chute and into our frustrated hands. Sometimes the coins wouldn't come back. This gave us an opportunity to practice a few favorite epithets. Occasionally native speakers would attempt to help us. One female campground manager held the belief that dumping all of our available coins into the telephone would give us the desired result. She took the phone, emptied our change purse, heard the rapid Italian, and shared our failure. Undaunted, she repeated the process. Her philosophical shoulder shrug emphasized for us the enormity of the problem we faced.

From this last experience with the campground manager, it should be clear that Hermes, the god of communication, had not picked us as the only ones to torture with telecommunications tribulations. Anything that was wired—hotel computers and fax machines, for example—was subject to sudden and inexplicable loss of service. Greece and southern Italy seemed particularly susceptible to Hermes' vagaries. For example, after telling us that the hotel accepted several credit cards, the clerk at the Athens Center Hotel informed us that his lines were down and we would have to check out with cash. The American Express office in Athens asked me to wait about fifteen minutes while permission was sought to grant me a cash advance on my card. After forty-five minutes, I asked for a decision. The clerk's accusatory look at the phone and comment that the line was down signaled that money would not be coming my way. As she executed the Greek shrug, I left.

Fortunately, in spite of Hermes' curses on regular phone service and institutional computers, he generally left e-mail and internet cafes alone. This communication link was the saving connection we needed to the U. S. We found the cafes to be like policemen. We could never find one when we really needed one, but otherwise we seemed to find them all the time. Further, because they are often imbedded in other establishments, signage was not always obvious. For instance, at Vieste, a small city on the eastern Point of the Gargano Promontory, we were delighted to learn that there was an Internet point. However, we were unable to find it from the directions given by an indifferent clerk at the town's visitors' bureau. A similarly indifferent policewoman told us the computers were in Bart's Bar, and she pointed in the general direction. After forty-five minutes, Nancy found the bar, more like a household garage, locked up tight. Typically, there were no signs indicating hours of business. Bart's might open at 5 PM or at 8 or it might be closed indefinitely. In any event we could not spend the day waiting for what might or might not happen. However, there were sufficient times when we did find access. The keyboards were often different, and the lines were sometimes quite slow, but the cost was very affordable—$4 to $5 an hour. In fact two of our hotels gave us free Internet access from the single computer they each had for this purpose.

In addition to his sins of omission and neglect, Hermes has also committed sins of commission. Chief among his mass communication transgressions is television. Like cocaine, television addiction and its attendant bizarre behaviors are alive and well in Italy and Greece just as they are in the U. S. There are plenty of stations available. High-volume commercials, game shows, sports reporting, and sensationalized news resound throughout the classical world. Like their U. S. counterparts, Italian and Greek bistros often feature numerous televisions, usually on different channels, operating mutely to provide distraction to otherwise unengaged patrons. Sometimes volume is played on one station—always much too loudly—to accompany one's meal and digestive processes. While this latter annoyance is not as prevalent as it is in the States, the signs are ominous, and it may not be long until like Coca Cola products, the television troglodytes have taken over nearly all of the public spaces in Europe.

Hermes, of course, is a pagan god, and some might wonder what the Catholic Church is doing to respond to these pagan transgressions. In fact, there has been some activity. Pope Pius XII, for example, tapped St. Clare, a thirteenth century colleague of St. Francis of Assisi, as the patron saint of television. Apparently, she is taking the Sodom and Gomorrah approach and waiting until things get really bad before she makes her move, just as Yahweh did in the Old Testament before he finally rained fire and brimstone on those two world-class cities of sin.

Radio and recorded music also suffer abuse in the hands of the sons and daughters of Hermes. Local and regional music is being supplanted by the constant cacophony of rock 'n' roll, a process of cultural deterioration much more advanced in Italy than in Greece. How odd and sad it is to sit in an Italian restaurant on the Mediterranean and have the room filled with songs by The Four Tops or Foreigner. Even worse is what happens when full Americanization takes place and hard rock at high volume fills the restaurant. Guitar runs and gastronomic enjoyment—this is a combination that only the criminally insane would maintain.

Yet, there is one area that is still immune from musical madness—the Italian and Greek campground. In the ten campgrounds Nancy and I stayed in, not once were we disturbed by the radio or sound system of another camper. When we considered the outrageous conduct that we've had to endure in American campgrounds, we found this to be an amazing blessing. Now, anyone who has not camped in a state campground might find the following incredible and think I'm exaggerating. Anyone who has camped will, I am sure, simply nod.

Nancy and I have been tent-camping since we married in 1968. Over the last ten years, we have visited state campgrounds with a pass one can obtain for those disabled. This can be a mixed blessing. One of the major problems in the campgrounds is that many campers seem totally oblivious of the noise they create. I suppose they think tent canvas is 100% effective as sound proofing. Now I expect that a group that arrives with jet-skis on a trailer will be noisy. They clearly don't have a clue. The sheer number of others equally brain-numb is astonishing. When a car stops at a campsite with car stereo blasting, it's only a nano-second before the boom box is blaring on the picnic table. Moments later a cooler overstuffed with beer cans joins the boom box. Within a half hour the campers—who weren't so bright in the first place—are on their way to noisy intoxication.

I remember a camper at a state park on Lake George one July 4th who thought the campground would benefit from an Eagles' concert at 1:30 in the morning. Fortunately, I was awake because the campers across from me had decided that 1 A.M. was a good time to split firewood! When we inspected the concert campsite the next day Nancy commented on a burial mound of beer cans that memorialized at least two cases!

I don't want to give the impression that state campgrounds are hell and private campgrounds are pastoral Arcady. They too can be victims of Hermes' hellions. At a campground near Bar Harbor, Nancy, my son Nick, and I were terrorized by a group of about twenty young people who drank to excess, fought with each other, abused women, and eventually pulled out a gun. Fortunately, I had sent Nancy and Nick away before the gun made its appearance, but knew if a tent didn't keep out noise, its chances of stopping a bullet were quite small. As a result. I spent most of the night trying to get below the grass roots beneath my tent.

From those and similar experiences it is easy to see why Nancy and I enjoyed our Greek and Italian camping. Clearly, we were not camping in high season, but there were other campers. The absence of Hermes' curse—the radio—was a gift of Zeus.

What wonderful places campgrounds in America would be if the first item that came out of the car was a piece of sporting equipment and not a boom box.

The charges, then, against Hermes are serious and many. Perhaps Zeus needs to spend less time changing himself into seductive coinage or deciding which animal would give him best cover for his amorous adventures and more time on doing periodic evaluations of his messenger minion.

CHAPTER 10

▼

DINING WITH DIONYSIUS

One of the advantages of being blind is that I'm freed from a lot of the distractions that befuddle my sighted friends. As a result I'm able to concentrate on the impressions of my other senses and to ruminate in a more focussed way about the events I experience. These abilities were chief among the reasons why I thought a trip to the Mediterranean would be worthwhile, even for someone like me with limited vision. From previous European experiences I knew that my senses of taste and smell would probably be fully involved in enjoying our travels. They certainly were.

However, before I begin to talk of the gifts of Dionysius—the food and drink of Italy and Greece—I must offer a disclaimer. I am not a gourmand. In fact, I don't know anyone who is. This is probably the case with most Americans, although we all know people who think they have gourmet sensibilities. When we ask these people about the quality of the food at a restaurant they just visited, they will describe the food as "very good" or "great." However, when Nancy and I sample the food, the best we can say is that it was edible or adequate or not unhealthy. It took me years to figure out why I got such unreliable reviews. It wasn't because these people had undeveloped taste buds and olfactory senses. No, it was a matter of making themselves look good and appear to be having a marvelous life experience. If they said they selected a restaurant, paid a reasonable sum, and had just adequate food, they would appear to be just a couple of average chumps. This is a realization they are not excited to admit; they're much more willing to give me a false report—about the food and about themselves.

Another factor may also be at work here. Americans, by and large, confuse quantity with quality. A "good" restaurant in America is one with big portions, slabs of meat, a bottomless salad bar, and "all you can eat." In the three months of our trip Nancy tells me that she did not see one "all you can eat" sign.

The signs we did see in Italy were reservation signs on tables. While the Greeks don't believe in reservations, the Italians have made reservations sacramental. It was not unusual for us to enter a nearly empty restaurant and find 90% of the tables reserved. Fortunately for us we always seemed to appear at restaurants just as they opened, 12:30 PM. for lunch and 7:30 for dinner. Since the prime dining time was an hour or more later, we were usually accommodated. One incident in particular makes this point quite well. We were staying in Via Reggio over the Easter weekend. We had spotted a restaurant near our hotel. Amazing to us, it did not open until 8:00 PM. When we walked in, the host told us that all the tables were reserved. My daughter, Nancy, and I must have presented such long faces and such downtrodden body language that the host came back to us and asked if we could eat in an hour and a half so the table would be available for the party who had reserved it for 9:30. I chuckled to myself and felt like saying, "Listen, we're Americans. We can probably be done in fifteen minutes. In fact, even at our biggest holiday dinner, Thanksgiving, most of us gobble the food down in less than a half hour." However, I kept my mouth shut, and we had a lovely dinner, finishing our meal in about an hour and twenty minutes.

During this meal, I, of course, had wine. Wine is one of the great Italian treats as well as one of the great Italian bargains. It is barely more expensive than bottled water, and a half liter of house red is about the same price as a single soda. Beer usually costs a bit more. During my two months in Italy I would say that the average price of a half liter of wine ranged between 4000 to 6000 lira—about $1.80 to $2.60 with the favorable exchange rate at the time. In the U. S. a single glass of similar wine—less than one-fourth of the amount—would cost from $2.25 to $4.50. Similar bargains in wine were also available in Greece. It's no wonder Dionysius and his Roman counterpart Bacchus were praised in classical antiquity.

Some might think that such inexpensive prices would lead to abuse. We found nothing of the sort. The consumption of wine, beer, and other alcoholic beverages is part of life from childhood. It is not a forbidden fruit. As a result people take it for granted. Having a glass of wine or a bottle of beer does not prove adulthood. It is just something that adds pleasure to life. Because it is not a forbidden fruit and always available, alcohol is used in moderation. People can purchase beer at McDonald's. Ice cream stands also feature a full array of liquor. Susie can have a double cone while Mom and Dad sip on a glass of wine and a scotch. It's all so civilized; further this abundance of choice puts out the message that people are free to make decisions and mature enough to make the right ones. I found it tremendously liberating after the repressive rules and regulations we've allowed our rulers–er, ah–legislators to impose upon us. This repression was crystallized when I came home and was not allowed to buy a six-pack of beer because my New York state I. D. had expired! I'm 54 years old, and although I think I could pass for 42—being blind keeps mirrors from being an enemy—there is no possibility I could be less than 21.

Such insulting ridiculousness makes me long for Europe. I'll always remember fondly taking my children to the animal petting area at the Madrid zoo in 1986. While they petted the animals in a fenced-in area, I sat on a stool at a small bar that stood right at the entrance to the petting area. I sipped a glass of wine for a half hour while they enjoyed themselves. It was life as the gods wanted it.

Experiences of a similar nature also caught my attention on this trip. At nearly every rest area along the extensive and magnificent autostrada system in Italy one can stop, eat, and enjoy a glass of wine or beer. In fact, there are often liquor stores attached to the highway restaurants. The message is sent: "You are a responsible and mature person." Those who abuse this freedom and respect are treated harshly. Lest I give the wrong impression, there are some limits. On the autostrada it is forbidden to sell or purchase beverages with more than a 20% alcohol content between the hours of 10 P.M. and 6 A.M. Whether this is the beginning of creeping repressionism and restriction, I don't know. What I do know is I felt free, and, like others around me, acted responsibly.

Wine was indeed the gift of the gods, yet the gods have certainly blessed Italy and Greece with other gifts that just did not make it into the canon of classical literature. Pizza, for one, is not prominently featured, but surely this Italian treasure must have come from Dionysius and Bacchus. The pizza in Italy is almost always very thin, much thinner than anything I've had in the states. The crust is seasoned deliciously and covered with a cornucopia of toppings. When I first arrived in Italy I often ordered the "fruta del mar" pizza, literally "fruit of the sea." I affectionately named this "garbage" pizza because the seafood that topped the pizza was served in its shells. Mussels, clams, and even a crustacean or two littered the thin surface. It was wonderful. Later I developed a liking for various vegetarian and four-cheese pizzas. The pizza in Italy is so good that it alone justifies a flight over. To illustrate how good the pizza is, I can even praise the frozen pizza. We bought several of these frozen pizzas from the coop grocery in Greve in Chanti. My daughter, Kate, cooked them, but I expected little. However, when I bit into the pizza, my tongue threw a party for my mouth. This stuff was as good as—or better—than the best pizza I had ever had in the States. The gods were wonderful. Yet, my faith was weak. I just couldn't accept the fact that this frozen pizza was so good. I doubted my own experience. As a result, we had the frozen pizza a second time. Again, the miracle occurred; again my taste buds said, "Hubba, hubba!"

Other foods were also found in the gods' treasure chest of chewables. The pastas, souvlaki, moussaka, and feta cheese were all among my favorites. I had been told that meat would be in short supply and expensive. Nonsense. Pork, veal, and beef were plentiful and quite affordable. Fish was a bit more expensive, especially octopus, but I'll never forget the thumb-thick tentacle I ate in Greece as an appetizer. It was cooked to a delicious tenderness and tasted like bald eagle.

Misting over all of this was olive oil, the cooking nectar of the gods. Its divine essence made nearly every dining experience a positive one. From haphazardly selected urban restaurants in Florence to beach front bistros on Mykonos to a campground cafe in Delphi, the quality of food and the joy of dining were high. Perhaps Athena had guided us to just the best places. If so, I owe her even more homage. However, I think the prayer of thanks and praise here more likely belongs to Dionysius. The patron of food and drink, he has set the foundation of simple pleasures that make the relaxed lifestyles of Italy and Greece a joy to behold and enjoy.

CHAPTER 11

▼

SCYLLA AND SILLIER

In <u>The Odyssey</u> the great Odysseus and his men face a tremendous navigation challenge as they attempt to pass through a narrow strait on their way back to Ithaca. On one side of the passage sits the dangerous whirlpool called Charybdis. If Odysseus' ship gets too close to this whirlpool, it will be sucked down, and the ship and all its crew will perish. However, if Odysseus guides his ship away from the whirlpool, it will be in proximity of Scylla, a six-headed monster who lives in a cave in a cliff that borders the sea. Each of the heads is able to reach out on a long neck and pluck sailors from their ships. In modern terms, Odysseus is between a rock and a hard place.

Travelers, too, must sail a very narrow path as they tell their stories. Some go abroad and only catalog reasons why the place they visited is inferior to the United States. Any feature that is different from the American way is negative. Change and diversity are undesirable. I often wonder why they travel at all, yet many of such an outlook do travel and do it often. As I have traveled the Mediterranean, I have witnessed numerous examples, especially among the Germans and the British, of a passion for sameness. German restaurants and tourist villages, British pubs and fish'n'chips take-outs are all attempts to make Spain, Italy, and Greece a bit more like Germany and Britain. In the U. S. the presence of lawns in Phoenix is a sure sign that people don't really want to be in a desert. What all of these groups want is better weather, not a different cultural or geographic experience. It just seems a shame to me that they spend so much money and do such a tremendous amount of environmental and cultural damage for the sake of a few degrees and a little sunshine. With a few lighting changes and a higher thermostat setting these folks would be much better off staying home.

Unfortunately, they do travel, often in RV's that will maintain the homey sameness they so desire. When they meet countrymen, the conversation is predictable, a nonstop harping about how the host country is different from—and inferior to—their home country. When they arrive home, this conversational diatribe continues, often, like Charybdis, sucking the life out of any dialogue and bringing everyone down. It's tedious, and so are they. It's a whirlpool of words that I have tried to avoid as a traveler.

On the other side are the travelers who take the opposite track and find nothing to complain about in their visited lands. Hopelessly Pollyannish and uncritical in their appraisals, these travelers seem not to use or need their heads at all. Symbolically, the Scylla snatches their heads as they travel much too close to the uncritical side of things. Like their opposites, these travelers quickly become tedious because of their lack of balance.

Some of those who hold the uncritical approach to travel must surely have been influenced by the contemporary assertion that all cultures and civilizations are somehow equal. To point out, therefore, how one culture or civilization is superior—in fact, to make any comparative claims at all—is insensitive to the cultures in question and very politically incorrect. Like the mandates of political correctness against being judgmental this caveat about cultures and civilizations is nonsense. One would have to be a non-thinker to accept it. For example, a culture or civilization that provides facilities to maintain the health of children is superior to those which do not. Cultures that mutilate the sexual organs of females are inferior to those that do not. Civilizations that provide secure and stable social frameworks are superior to those that do not. There are, of course, limitless criteria one can apply to develop a matrix of comparison.

It is in this light of critical analysis that I offer the following observations on the countries I have visited. I have tried to steer a balanced course in my comments thus far, offering praise where warranted and blame where required. Here I hope to catalog some of the more outrageous and befuddling aspects of the places we experienced.

1. I've heard of the paperless office—but the paperless toilet? Greece's ubiquitous insistence on not flushing toilet paper but rather placing the used paper in a waste basket simply must go. There's no reason for it that makes sense. I've heard suggestions that the plumbing can't accommodate the paper and that the water supply is insufficient, but both of these reasons fail to stand up under scrutiny. Sicily and Spain have no problem flushing, and their water situations are similar. I did stay at a campground and an apartment where flushing the paper was permissible. If it could happen there, it should happen everywhere. To get motivated all one has to do is to encounter an overflowing wastebasket in a restroom on public transportation. Yikes!

2. Somehow, Italians have to have their consciousness raised about the value of a queue. Now I know lining up means that someone will be last, but this doesn't mean someone is less of a person. It's only a temporal thing. One merely arrived after others. Amazingly the Italians have turned the simple and efficient line into a face and esteem exercise. As a result little old women form aggressive mobs at bus doors. Ordering food in a delicatessen or cafeteria becomes a competition, a prelude to indigestion. If one adds a little sexism to the Italian diversion to lines, the Segesta syndrome occurs. Nancy and I were waiting to buy admission tickets to this marvelous archaeological site. We were behind some Italian women. As they approached the ticket clerk, their

male companions, who had been sitting on the sidelines, jumped up and took the places of the women to make the ticket transaction. Exchanging money for tickets had some significance and showed power and authority. The men would do that. Standing in line was for the inferiors; the women did that. In this episode Nancy and I saw firsthand the repulsion that exists for the concept of lining up. Nonetheless, Italy needs to see the light and get in line with other countries.

3. Marilyn Monroe once starred in a movie <u>Some Like It Hot</u>. When it comes to food, I would say that most like it hot. However, many Greeks seem to be fans of the lukewarm. As a diner at lunch and dinner I'm not sure when I eat a lukewarm meal if it has been properly prepared. Further, I wonder whether the food has been left out at room temperature for a long while and the indigenous bacteria are holding a convention. Fortunately, there is a way to convey one's desire to step up the temperature. By saying, "zesto," as one orders a meal, the waiter will know that the meal should be hot. Although saying the word, "zesto," makes me laugh, it's a small price to pay to get food the way I will enjoy it.

4. In both Italy and Greece, road signage is plainly silly. In Italy there are too many signs; in Greece there are hardly any. Moreover, in both countries, highway officials treat their roadways as secret agents; they refuse to disclose their identities.

In Italy, traffic circles are frequent and consistent; they are all confusing. Each auto octopus has at least four roads attached to it. Many of these monsters display six or seven roadway tentacles. At each highway option stand several posts, each of which is adorned with ten signs. One of these traffic trees will list all the towns that may theoretically be reached by taking a particular road. I say theoretically because many of the towns listed are not actually on the road. However, they are in the general vicinity. Thus, the same town can actually be on several signs. In fact, during our trip Nancy would occasionally come to a "T" intersection where both a left and right turn would get one to the same place.

As she progressed through the circle Nancy would try to read the forest of traffic trees planted along her way. She would try to ignore the trees that listed businesses, restaurants, and hotels. She would try to visualize a map and imagine which road, passing near all the named towns, would lead us to our destination, which unfortunately was often not listed on any sign. At the same time Italian drivers, some of whom actually knew where they were going, would buzz in and out of the grip of the octopus like small fish, not large enough to be bothered with. We were the main prey, the two Americans in the massive Peugeot 406 traveling slowly and cautiously. The absence of route numbers produced an inky indecision that forced Nancy to take a deep breath whenever we entered the tortuous tentacles. I, of course, sat blind, helpless, and quiet, silently cheering her on, yet waiting for the thump of steel that would indicate Athena had left us. The goddess, however, never abandoned us.

5. Any first-time traveler to Europe is immediately taken by its smells. The fragrances of garlic, fish, and olive oil all waft through the streets, carried along by Mediterranean breezes. These, of course, are the pleasant odors. There also lurks among the cobbled stones and quaint buildings quite a different smell—sewer gas. In old cities you have old sewer systems. Old sewer systems belch gas. This wouldn't be a problem if it weren't for the fact that eating on the street is so popular and so enjoyable. In Pisa I remember being almost bowled over by an invisible cloud of gas on the periphery of a pastry shop where delicate flavors and subtle fragrances were the foundations of delight. In Napflion in Greece, Nancy and I frequented a street of restaurants. Each of these eateries served delicious food. All of them were close enough to sewer outlets that, depending on the wind, could cause considerable interference with one's dining enjoyment. For us part of the process of

table selection was judging the wind and its direction. This information would dictate whether we dined inside or outside.

Unlike farmers who grow used to the pungent odor of manure, the waiters at these restaurants were quite cognizant of the sewer smell. A slight change in wind direction could greatly decrease the number of diners and thereby affect their tips. The town, after all, was full of restaurants. As a result the waiters made primitive moves to counteract the smell. One day we saw one inserting a carefully cut piece of corrugated cardboard over the sewer opening. Simple as it was, it probably was quite effective. In any case, after this experience, the smell of sewer gas inevitably prompted Nancy to ask me, "Is it time to eat?"

6. One of the things that Nancy most enjoys is a cafeteria line. Seeing a broad array of food, especially desserts, spread out before her gives her a range of selection she particularly enjoys. In a country like Italy, where our knowledge of the language was so limited, the cafeteria line would presumably give us the opportunity to point at what we wanted rather than to guess at a menu. It sounds fine in theory, but surprisingly, some Italian cafeterias do not work this way. The cafeteria at the Segesta Archaeological site in Sicily is a case in point. Instead of pointing to food, placing it on our tray, and paying for it, we were forced to look at the food and then go to the cashier to tell her what we were going to get. She then rang up our order and gave us a receipt. We then went back to the cafeteria line, handed the receipt to the food attendant and received our meal. Obviously, whoever designed this system was seriously demented. With people coming and going through the food line—some to look and some to obtain—the traffic flow was horrendous. Also, with the Italian aversion to lines, the area around the cashier quickly seemed more like the trading pit at a stock market than part of a restaurant. Our paucity of vocabulary to describe the food we wanted didn't help our situation nor that of the other tourists in the restaurant. While some apparently delicious food was available, people were often reduced to ordering pizza, pannini (sand-

wiches), and wine because these were the words most people knew. Occasionally an adventurous soul would order an item from a sign on the wall, not knowing exactly what the item was. Upon receipt of this order, the adventurous diner would stare at the braised cow's stomach in front of him in much the same way a young child might stare at a whole boiled lobster.

The pattern of "tell and get" occurred several times in our cafeteria excursions. Each time it was chaotic, and each time it left us scratching our heads and usually eating pizza.

7. What anyone with limited language skills counts on in foreign travel is the ability to be interpersonally dramatic, to play charades to convey basic meaning. Sometimes this is actually a lot of fun for both participants. Unfortunately, technology and automation are putting an end to traveler charades. We found this to be horribly true at toll booths, both on the highway and at airports.

After picking up our daughter Kate and our car at the Milan airport, we set off for Lago Maggiore, about forty kilometers or so. We quickly came to a highway toll booth. It had no attendant, but it did have one of those barrier arms that would keep us from moving forward until we had completed a successful transaction. As we stopped, a mechanical female voice shot forth a barrage of words in rapid-fire succession. The three of us quickly agreed that she had a "thank you" at the end. We had no other clue. After a few seconds the insistent clatter of the message started again. Once more, we gained little comprehension. Fortunately, Kate, who had that semester of Italian in her cranium, started to piece together some of the information on the side of the automated booth. She asked for my credit card. I was somewhat reluctant. I wasn't ready to have one of my three cards eaten up in my first hour on the road. When the voice clatter of the machine started again, I quickly gave up my card. Nancy put it in a slot, the gate went up, the card came back, our $2 was paid, and our mechanical friend sang out, "Arrividerci!"

From this experience we discovered that putting credit cards in slots, through risky, would often silence the voices of mechanical martinets. We became complaisant and developed a certain hubris concerning toll booth transactions. This hubris would come back to torment us a few months later when we picked up our son at the Rome airport.

First, I must say that I was impressed by the Rome airport. It was large, modern, and clean. There was one troubling aspect about it, however; it suffers from an identity crisis. The official name of the airport is Leonardo Da Vinci airport. The locals, highway signs, and even computerized travel itineraries refer to it as Fumisano Airport. This is absolutely crazy. Imagine the shock we had, when not knowing of the airport's dual identity, we looked at Nick's itinerary the day before we were to pick him up and found he was landing at Fumisano and not Da Vinci. Imagine further our anxiety when we couldn't locate this airport on our map. Eventually, one of Nancy's guidebooks revealed the identity craziness. But why does such a potential problem continue? New York City isn't putting up highway signs directing people to Idlewild, the old name of JFK Airport. Travelers need simplicity, not confusion.

Nonetheless, we did meet Nick and were pulling out of a paid parking area. Nancy had picked up a ticket upon entering, and we approached the toll gate hoping to find an attendant. There wasn't one. Yet, we thought we were ready. I had lots of change, small bills, and, of course, several credit cards. We would show our somewhat sophisticated son that his parents weren't country bumpkins after all, that not only did we know our way around the block, we knew our way around the world. With the confidence of Oedipus solving a riddle, Nancy placed her parking stub in the slot. Surprisingly, it came back, and the mechanical matron repeated her mantra, although I thought I heard a tone of annoyance in her mechanical voice. Nancy assumed that there was just a slight technical glitch and repeated the process. Again the stub was rejected. Now, angry words began to be directed toward the machine. Like people raising their voices in a foreign country when they are not understood we insisted that the machine would read our stub and give us a bill we would gladly pay. We kept hearing words that referred to some ticket or receipt, and so Nancy kept stuffing that stub into that bulimic slot.

Finally, we decided that the booth was defective and we went to another lane. Again we heard the maddening mantra. At last Nancy backed out of this lane too, and we sat frustrated, ready to spit or to gouge out someone's eyes, we were so angry.

Our son, who had just landed in Rome, must have wondered how his parents had survived in Europe for so many weeks when they apparently could not make their way out of a public parking lot. I suppose that this wonder about our survival might have led him to a greater spirituality, for there surely must be some force guiding or protecting us. We clearly could not make it on our own.

Perhaps, then, it was this protective spirit that inspired Nancy to park the car and go back into the terminal. She would find someone who would unravel this riddle of parking lot departure. Sure enough, she located a cashier window inside with an automated payment machine just to the right. She inserted our stub and then the required lira. In return she received a new stub, the paper key to our freedom.

8. Near the end of our stay Nancy and I pulled into a rather upscale campground on Lake Lugano. It had a lovely pool side restaurant, several bars, a large store, and a variety of bungalows. Although we had no reservation the reception clerk was able to place us in a two-bedroom mobile home. As we unpacked, Nancy found the invoice for the mobile home. It had been delivered just a month before we arrived. Nancy guessed that we were the second occupants.

As we were settling in, the manager came over to welcome us. He apologized for the fact that we had no furniture for the covered verandah that was attached to the trailer. He assured us in the most vigorous way that a complete set of outdoor furniture would be ours before nightfall. We were grateful. He seemed very proud of the trailer. He especially drew our attention to the freestanding air conditioner that stood in the main living area. With the greatest pride he demonstrated its operation. Since it was going to be sunny and hot, I took comfort in knowing we had such a modern convenience to keep us cool.

When the manager left, we turned on the air conditioner and did some final house keeping chores. After about twenty minutes, Nancy declared she was going to sit outside. Putting my hand to the cool outflow of the air conditioner, I told her I would stay inside. The room had not cooled off, but I optimistically assured her that within just a few minutes, the room would be quite comfortable. After thirty-two years of marriage, Nancy has become quite familiar with this Pollyanna-ish side of my personality. She wiped the beaded sweat from her forehead and said, "I'm going outside." I was disappointed by her lack of faith. Sitting on the couch next to the air conditioner, I felt like a poker player who had just drawn four of a kind. I couldn't wait to play my hand and show it off. Surely the room temperature would fall to 72 degrees, and I would call her in. "See, Nancy," I would say, "isn't it cool in here?"

However, as the minutes passed, it didn't seem to be getting any cooler. If anything, it seemed to be getting hotter. I put my hand over the overflow. The air was coming out fresh and cool. Why wasn't the room cooling down? All the windows were closed. What could be going on? I leaned back on the couch feeling somewhat deflated. My four of a kind seemed more like a pair of deuces. Suddenly I felt a blast of hot air like the breath of Beelzebub. Where was it coming from? My hand traced the hellish current until it came to a large opening—at the back of the air conditioner! Mirabile dictu (wondrous to say), the staff at the campground had "installed" the air conditioner without venting it. This heat exchanger blew cool air from the front and hot air from the back. It wasn't even an equal trade. Because of the energy involved in making the exchange, the air conditioner was probably adding heat to the room. I didn't even have a pair of deuces.

I looked for a hole in the wall or some flexible ventilator pipe to complete the installation myself, but none was to be found. There was no point going to the manager. We had been in Italy long enough to know that work of this kind never occurred instantly. In fact, the enthusiastically promised verandah furniture never arrived. When we bumped into the manager he would promise that it would come, but it never happened. I don't think that this makes him a promise breaker. In the Mediterranean region I've noticed that promises are statements of intent and not commitments to action as they are here in the U. S. The manager really wished for us to be comfortable, and his promises were the articulation of his wishes. I appreciated the kindness of his thoughts.

9. When Nancy and I first visited Europe together in the early 70's, jokes about European body odor were commonplace. The authentic smell of other human beings was markedly present, much more so than it was even in the New York City subways. In addition, the knockout fumes of cheap cologne and perfume seemed to invade any air not already occupied by that odor so human. Part of the reason for this omnipresent odor was the lack of convenient washing facilities. A good shower was very much the exception rather than the rule. Plumbing, water heating facilities, and spaces for installation all had costs that many Europeans could just not absorb. Today, there is a more prosperous Europe, but some of the shower facilities I encountered were just bizarre.

Once one decides to install a shower system, the question becomes whether one is going to enclose the showering person to keep water from inundating the rest of the bathroom. The aqua optimists think that just a flexible hose with shower head attached will be sufficient. Sometimes these are placed in bathtubs. This configuration promotes either a trip to the chiropractor or a romantic interlude. To keep water in the tub, one has to keep low. Keeping low and manipulating the shower head in the confines of a tub inevitably lead to strained muscles and skeletal misalignment. However, the floor does stay pretty dry. I always preferred getting help—the romantic approach. Here I can concern myself with body positioning and soap location while Nancy concerned herself with water containment and shower head direction.

Some places had a flexible hose setup on the wall but no tub. There was usually a drain in the middle of the bathroom floor. Sometimes a one-inch high tile border would dictate where the showerer was supposed to confine himself and his water. In this latter case a drain would be within the boundary. In any case, water went everywhere. Even with the most careful and delicate of movement, the rainy ricochet would drench most of the room. This certainly dampened our enthusiasm and our clothing for using the sink or toilet after the showering activity.

The most bizarre of the open-face showering opportunities occurred when we confronted a shower head permanently affixed to the wall. Here there was no pretext of possible moisture containment. If we wanted to shower, we were going to saturate the entire room. It felt odd to proceed this way, but we knew we didn't want to be stinkin' Americans, so we let the drops fall where they may.

Fortunately, for our psychological comfort many of the places we stayed did not subscribe to the open-face shower method. The majority of these offered the shower curtain as the containment device. Unfortunately, most of the curtain structures seem designed for an anorexic teenager. The curtains almost always touched my body. The thinner curtains would actually adhere to my flesh as if I were wearing a plastic jumpsuit. I found this neither pleasant nor sanitary as I was continuously making contact with the soap scum of the past.

A few times there were actually shower stalls, and Nancy and I relished them even if we had to keep our elbows relatively close to our sides as we washed. Our hotel in Aqui-Terme, Italy, had one of the best showers of our entire stay. As the commercial for the Baseball Hall of Fame suggests, "It's a memory that will last forever."

The scylla I've described here had eight heads, 33 1/3 % more than the creature who confronted and consumed members of Odysseus' crew. Nonetheless, my monster, like that of Odysseus, was not able to force me to the negativity of Charybdis. While the silliness was real, it was more than compensated for by the positive richness of the places I visited and the people I met. This richness was the wind that filled my sails and kept me on course.

CHAPTER 12

▼

THE LEGACY OF
POLYPHEMUS

In human and mythological history, legacies fall into two kinds—positive and negative. The legacy of Penelope, for example, is her vibrant and compelling illustration of the faithful wife. Strong and clever, Penelope is faithful both because of her love for Odysseus and because such faithfulness is an essential element of her integrity. As an exemplar of spousal fidelity, Penelope has a fame that has lasted for nearly three thousand years.

Richard Nixon and Bill Clinton, on the other hand, have left behind negative legacies. Their stories of political corruption and deceit have become models for what not to do as a public official. In this way their legacies have some value, although they surely are not to be thanked for their examples of egregious impropriety.

Polyphemus, the cyclops sired by Poseidon, is a similar producer of a negative legacy. Polyphemus violated the sacred code of Xenia, or hospitality. When Odysseus and his men asked the one-eyed giant for food and shelter, something quite appropriate for a traveler to do, Polyphemus began to eat them! This kind of behavior and perversion of the concept of hospitality would even be censured in France. In islands of the Mediterranean such behavior is anathema, and Polyphemus pays dearly when the wily Odysseus must blind Polyphemus in order to save his men and escape.

Yet, the legacy of Polyphemus is a valuable lesson. The gods hate the inhospitable, and the people of the Mediterranean know this so very well. As Nancy and I made our journey, the hospitality we were shown constantly gratified and amazed us.

At the Hotel Milton in Rimini, for example, the desk clerk welcomed us with such warmth that one would think we were cherished regulars—we had never been there before. At Greve in Chianti in Tuscany, we ate in a budget restaurant crowded with teens who made about the same amount of noise as students in a junior high school cafeteria the day before Christmas vacation. As we were leaving after the meal, Nancy, Kate, and I were all given complimentary liqueurs. The hostess offered this gesture as a way of thanking us for our tolerance. It wasn't necessary for her to do this, but it certainly was a gracious thing to do.

In Aqui Terme, a lovely little town outside of Genoa, Nancy and I stayed in a simple hotel. We decided to dine in the hotel restaurant. Eventually we were the only diners in the restaurant, yet we received such fine food and enthusiastic service that we couldn't have done better if we were the Duke and Duchess of York.

Outside of Agrigento we stayed for several nights in a bungalow in a fairly low-level campground. Drainpipes on the outdoor wash basins were broken and poured water near our feet. Other outdoor basins had weeds growing up out of the drains. An abandoned car lacking a few doors occupied one of the tent sites. Yet, in this rather unappealing location, we met one of the most interesting people of our trip, a young carpenter from Germany named Michael. Michael was accompanied by an attractive and lovely girl named Fanny. Despite some resistance from Fanny, Michael was hoping to woo her and win her as his wife. Why he had brought her to this campground to complete such a romantic mission remains to this day beyond the comprehension of either Nancy or me. Michael, nonetheless, was sure of his plan. One night he invited Nancy and me to join him and Fanny at a friend's seafood restaurant. Our host Giuseppa presented us with a magnificent meal. During the progress of the courses he and his son sat with us. We all drank some of the fine wine Michael had purchased before we entered the restaurant. Michael showed some impressive language skills as he launched forth on various topics, speaking to Fanny in German, Giuseppa and his son in Italian, and Nancy and me in English. At about 11 PM when Giuseppa's son presented Michael with the bill, Michael asserted, "This is no time to talk about money." In fact, from this point on, Michael pointed out how inappropriate it was that we had even been billed at all! Giuseppa and his son had drunk Michael's wine; Michael and his friends had consumed Giuseppa's food. As far as Michael was concerned, everything was even. Apparently, Michael must have convinced Guiseppa, for he rescinded the check. We left, leaving behind a handsome gratuity and even handsomer gratitude.

After leaving Sicily and Italy, we arrived in the vicinity of Delphi in Greece. Our accommodation was another campground, but this time we were going to stay in the tent we had brought with us. Our site was a few steps from the pool and on the edge of a cliff that afforded, I am told, a panoramic view of the hills and the sea. As we got ready to cook meals, we brought out the large gas cylinder we had purchased in Sicily. Try as we could, we could not remove the covering on the gas opening. Nancy took the cylinder to the office. Again, Xenia made itself known. The office manager attacked the problem with gusto and tried several tools. Finally he was able to free up the gas. He charged nothing. His reward was a couple of happy campers.

At another campground—this time in Rafina—we were permitted to store our car for the most modest of charges. On Mykonos we were driven free of charge back and forth to the port. At rental properties in Napflion, Greece, and Belagio, Italy, our hosts welcomed us with drinks, bottles of wine, and home-cooked meals of very fine quality. The instances of kindness and consideration were so numerous that they might seem exaggerated. They weren't, and it was this sense that we were welcome and cared for that added so much to our comfort level and the success of the trip.

One final experience will encapsulate the tremendous hospitality shown to us. On our way from Napflion to Athens we stopped to visit an archaeological site at Numeia. There is a fine ancient stadium here, good remnants of baths and a superior museum developed with American funding and the expertise of the University of California. After a few hours visiting the site, Nancy and I set off for Athens, but lunch was the immediate focus of our attention and our stomachs. It was about 1:30 in the afternoon. At first our prospects seemed very bleak. Few buildings of any sort were visible, and traffic on the road we had chosen was simply nonexistent. Nancy began to recite the inventory of edibles available in the car. We had nuts, post-ripe fruit, crackers, month-old breadsticks, a tin or two of some Greek specialty we had picked up in the market, and perhaps some bread remnants if we searched under our baggage or in the trunk. To go with the bread, there was, of course, always a large quantity of bottled water. None of this sounded very appetizing to me at the moment.

As I began to reach for the nuts, Nancy declared, "There's a place." We made a U-turn and pulled into a place that seemed like a mini-resort in the middle of nowhere. Nancy described a large building, a big swimming pool, and a parking lot crammed with cars.

When we entered expectant and hungry, our hopes for food were somewhat dashed. Nancy informed me that the entire restaurant seemed reserved for a private party—a double baptism it turned out. However, both of us decided to look pathetic and stay in the entrance way. Perhaps we could get a bite at the bar—anything other than the bread scraps beckoning in the car.

At this point a member of the staff approached us and, much to our surprise, sat us at a vacant table. Apologetically, she conveyed to us that we would only be able to eat the same menu as the party participants—roast pork, Greek salad and broiled potatoes. What a shame! Nancy and I both feasted on great food, salad, and wine. The cost for both of us was 5500 drachma—about $14.50.

Our gastronomic needs satisfied, Nancy watched the family festivities. She looked intently as numerous family members got up and performed various folk dances. Numerous rhythms and melodies resounded in the hall. Young and old alike partook in the Dionysian celebration. Here was folk dancing—not in a tourist nightclub, but authentic and as real as it gets. Nancy was entranced by the sights, and I was caught up in the intoxicating sounds of the music that kept unfolding.

Suddenly, two well-dressed men approached our table, carrying a carafe of wine. "Would you honor us by taking a glass of wine?" one of the men asked. As I pushed my glass forward, both men sat down. They were close relatives of the baptized children, and one spoke excellent English. He told us that he had earned a sociology degree from the University of London. His companion, he told us, did not speak English but wanted to welcome us—obvious strangers—to Greece and to the reception.

As my glass was again filled, I told our generous friends why we were in Greece. I mentioned that among the few Greek words I knew was the word Xenia, meaning hospitality. I said that since the time of the ancients, Greeks had been known for their hospitality, and here and now was a modern day example. This was conveyed to the Greek speaker, who broke into a smile. His next words were then translated for me. He apologized that he only spoke Greek and couldn't welcome me to his country in English. I replied that it is I who should apologize since I am visiting his country where the language is, of course, Greek. Once I said those words, firm and enthusiastic handshakes flew fast and furious. We drained several carafes and talked for about an hour. When we left, I felt more like a relative leaving a family party than a stranger in a strange land. I'm sure Zeus was pleased with the Xenia I had found.

CHAPTER 13

▼

TRAVELING WITH ATHENA

My wife Nancy is an extraordinary person, although it would take much cajoling for her to admit she was very special. Let me cite just two examples. In 1986 we took a five-month trip to Europe. The trip began in January in Luxembourg, included nearly four months on the Costa del Sol in Spain, and ended with a month of camping that returned to Luxembourg via Switzerland. We took this trip with an eleven-year-old daughter and a four-year-old son. Nancy, somehow, was able to pack for the three seasons of this trip so that we were able to traverse the Paris Metro and the Madrid subways with all our bags in our own hands! It was a miracle of organization, preparation, and compactness. I'm sure any woman who has faced a similar challenge would recognize the magnitude of this accomplishment.

In 1993 Nancy displayed an entirely different kind of specialness. A week before we were scheduled to leave for five months in England, she was diagnosed with breast cancer. She convinced her surgeon to postpone surgery for three and a half weeks, so she could set up my son and me in England where she planned to rejoin us as soon as her operation and radiation treatments were completed. Within three weeks of her surgery, she was photographed cross-country skiing through the streets of Cortland, New York, after a major snow storm. Although Nancy's radiation kept her away longer than anticipated, she rejoined my son and me in Spain in early May.

As I look back at the experience it is now clear to me that Athena had tied herself to our journey even during the planning stages. For instance, she must have had a role in Nancy's acceptance of a purchase/repurchase agreement for our car while in Europe. Although willing to take risks, Nancy is not foolhardy. I remember quite distinctly how I lay on the living room floor with my back against the sofa while Nancy slowly read every word of the automobile contract in her hand before she signed a promissory note for $24,000 on a car she had never seen with a company whose office she had never visited. Other people may do this routinely. Not us. As a result, our financial life is rather simple and stressless. This was different. Yet, somehow, guided by a force not usually present in our house, Nancy signed.

Obviously, even from just these two examples, it is clear that Nancy possesses special gifts—gifts for which I thank the gods. Yet, even these gifts exist within the realm of human possibility. In our trip to Italy and Greece another power—another protector—was present.

When we arrived at the Milan airport the rest of the car drama unfolded. Much to our relief, we did meet a woman carrying a placard with Nancy's name. Nancy and this woman, who spoke hardly any English, went out to hand over the car and explain its operation. After approximately ten minutes of pointing at papers, getting Nancy's signature on unreviewed documents, and showing us that the steering wheel turned, our Italian orientation representative handed Nancy the keys and disappeared into the throng of airport travelers. I glanced at my wife. She is, as I said, special, but how could she deal with this—a strange car, a strange country, a strange language, and what were reported to be some of the most dangerous roads in the industrialized world? To top it all off, her first driving experience was to be on airport roads in a new car she had paid $22,000 for after a night on a plane without sleep! I wouldn't have blamed her if she would have sat down and cried. Yet, she only said, "You'd think they'd send someone who could speak a little English." With that she jumped into the driver's seat, fumbled with a few controls, and off we went. Surely, she was divinely inspired. How else could she manage such a superhuman performance?

Yet, this was just the beginning of Athena's care. After touring mainland Italy for three weeks, we took the overnight ferry from Genoa to Palermo, Sicily. Although we had anticipated arriving in Palermo in daylight at 7 PM, we actually arrived in rainy darkness at 9:30 PM. Nancy drove us off the ship as we looked for overnight accommodations. In a matter of minutes we were outside the city on a road heavily under construction.

The rain made it even more difficult to see in the unlit darkness. The road zigzagged unpredictably around construction barriers. We drove for several miles but nothing approaching a possible accommodation was visible. Nancy and I could feel each other's tension. We said little, for saying, "I really don't like this" more than once is amply redundant and amplifies the fear. We did agree to turn around and head back to Palermo. The confused nature of the construction detours made the return trip just as terrifying as the ride out. Nancy swerved around construction barrels, wondered about the meaning of signs, and expressed hope that she could keep the car on the roadway and not end up in a ditch.

Then, in a miracle of peripheral vision, she exulted, "I think I just saw a sign for a hotel!" Again, she turned the car around. "I think I see some lights way up that hill." With that she retraced our passage and put us on something more like a driveway than a roadway that carried us up a half mile to safety and sleep.

We had seen no lights on the hillside until we had turned around. In the next day's light, the sign indicating the hotel's presence was only about the size of three business envelopes. Yet, in some miraculous way, Nancy had been able to look at the precise point through the darkness at just the right moment. Athena had surely guided her eyes.

From this point on, Athena made herself much more visible. In fact, the next night we stayed—by chance as we thought—at Camping Athena. However, in many of our subsequent travels, Athena's presence by name, by temple, and by intervention became too much a part of our journey to be just circumstantial.

When we arrived in Greece, we knew that the stakes, in terms of travel difficulties, had risen appreciably. Not only the language was different, so also was the alphabet. The roads are the most dangerous in Europe. In addition, the country itself was not modern, like Italy. It was clearly a step below on the industrialization scale, still obviously uncomfortable with computers, time management, and personal regimentation. While I was glad to see the Greeks fight so hard against technological conformity and the loss of their individualistic souls, I knew that as foreigners Nancy and I would have to work a bit harder here to carry on our journey. Yet this was the nation favored by Athena and the cradle of Western Civilization. I was thrilled to breathe its air.

After several weeks on the mainland we decided to visit a few islands. We went to the small coastal town of Tolo, a few kilometers from Napflion, to arrange for our passage. It was here that Athena embraced us.

It was a lovely May day. We had explored the waterfront portion of the town and were walking past several blocks of restaurants and shops. We would stay on the sidewalk unless people, plants, signage, or merchandise forced us into the narrow street. At this point we were walking on the sidewalk on the sea side of the street when Nancy, with me on her elbow, stepped down into the street. After about thirty feet, I heard the thundering sound of a truck engine—a very large truck engine. "Get back! Get on the curb! Quick!" Nancy shouted. I jumped back to what I thought was the safety of the curb and sidewalk. The truck careened past us, missing us by a few inches. Even as it passed, I made no further move to step back. A presence held me secure in that spot.

Nancy muttered, "What an idiot! He almost hit us!" Then, unexpectedly and suddenly, she yelled at me, "Dan, don't move!" I didn't; I just stayed frozen where I was—something I had learned as a good thing to do whenever people warn me.

"Why? What's wrong?" I said.

"Just take my hand and step slowly forward," Nancy advised.

After I was on the street, Nancy asked if I knew what I was standing on. I told her I thought I was on the curb that was part of a sidewalk in front of a store. There was no store, and there was no sidewalk, she informed me. There was just a wide curb. Had I taken a step back I would have fallen almost ten feet and landed, probably on my back, on some seaside boulders. At best I would have broken my back; at worst I would have fractured my skull and died.

Realizing this, I began to tremble and felt faint. I shuddered to think how close, how very close, I had come to disaster. It wasn't Nancy's fault, to be sure. The truck had appeared so suddenly. Why hadn't I stepped back? After all, I thought there was a sidewalk there. A force had kept me on the curb, and I knew who it was.

Oddly enough, after this experience I was more optimistic about my personal safety rather than less. After all, there was clearly a goddess protecting me. I knew that the goddess could not alter my destiny or fate, but she might be able to delay it somewhat if it were tragic. Athena could also, if she wished, avert any gratuitous moments of suffering that could be cast upon me by envious gods. With Nancy on one side of me and Athena on the other, I felt charmed.

Several weeks later we headed for Patras. We had been in the mountains at Kalvarita, the birthplace of modern Greek independence. We had all day to traverse the forty kilometers or so to Patras, so Nancy decided she would like to drive the mountain roads to get a better look at the country. We had a good map, lots of gas, and plenty of time.

Things went quite well for awhile. We passed magnificent flowering fields, unspoiled villages, and even a few road signs. After awhile, however, all signage disappeared. Nonetheless, we were still descending. This reassured us; we were headed for the sea.

After about thirty minutes, we were no longer descending. In fact we were ascending again! We hadn't seen any villages in awhile, and there was no traffic or road signs. We had a little compass, but it was useless. The road seemed to turn 360 degrees as it made its way around the mountain heights. First, it would turn clockwise for a little while, then counterclockwise.

The silence we had shared around Palermo returned again. It was now lunch time, and the stale crackers and leftover nuts from a Kalvarita bar tasted pretty good. For the only time in our trip we were hopelessly lost, and I was beginning to worry about making our ferry connection. After all, we could have spent the last hour traveling away from Patras.

Nancy and I exchanged ideas about what to do. We could go ahead and hope to come to a town or major—and marked—intersection. We could try to retrace our steps. Although we were both anxious, we were not in a state of panic—yet. We still had gas; we still had time; it was a beautiful day.

We thought about our options, and Nancy kept the car rolling along the deserted highway. Suddenly, Nancy blurted out, "Look at that snake!" She then described a large snake that was crossing the highway in front of us. We stopped. Nancy formed a course of action. We would proceed forward but ask for help if we saw another human being.

About a kilometer later Nancy hit the brakes and bounded out of the car with map in hand. I admired the way she left the car after seeing that snakes were in the vicinity. I had no intention of ever getting out of the car again.

She returned with information and a plan. The man she had seen in his yard off the road spoke no English, but the map provided common ground. Forty-five minutes later we were in the outskirts of Patras.

Had Athena sent the snake to force a decision? Was that really a country resident in his yard or Athena in one of her many disguises? All I know is that we were delivered from hopelessness and anxiety by a snake and a stranger in a matter of minutes.

We then took the overnight ferry to Brindisi at the heel of Italy. Our goal was the spur on the Italian boot, the Gargano promontory. It was a long ride, and we stopped along the way to see the Trulli houses in Alberbello. By the time we arrived in the area of the promontory it was already late afternoon.

The Gargano promontory is a massive outcropping of mountain and rock that juts out into the Adriatic. Roughly circular, it is about 35 kilometers in diameter. Our destination was Vieste, its easternmost point. There is a winding road around the rim of the promontory. There is a very winding road through its center. We decided to take what the map showed as the less winding road.

Those familiar with California's Coastal Highway will have some idea of Gargano's rim road. On one side of the road is a precipitous drop into the sea; on the other side is an intruding cliff that seems to have desires about blocking the road. Like the Coastal Highway, the road weaves back and forth. Those acquainted with the Amalfi Drive outside of Naples would call it a corniche. Such roads are obviously dangerous. The driver must concentrate or crash. In addition, the driver must be ready for cars coming in the other direction where scenery might overcome sense, and contemplation might supplant concentration.

It was all as dangerous as we could wish. However, when we got about ten kilometers from Vieste the danger became incredible. Instead of just twisting, the road began to rise and fall in steep climbs and sharp descents. Intermittent canopies of heavy foliage cut off the sun in a deep shade and then suddenly opened up for the road to explode in glaring brilliance. Frequently the twists and grades would bring our windshield directly facing the early evening sun. Then, suddenly, we'd drop and turn into almost nocturnal darkness. Indeed, the changes were like those of an electrical storm at night, yet, in reality, it was still daylight.

Cars bunched, passed, and accelerated as if the existence of an afterlife were a sure thing. Nearly every vehicle had at least one tire on the center dividing line. Half of the vehicles coming the other way were clearly over the line; a few were in the wrong lane as they tried to cut the turn.

The presence of insect innards all over our windshield created a distracting barrier to the frightening reality in which we moved. How long could it take to go ten kilometers? What would it be like when we crashed?

I had assumed that we would crash but then, after twenty-five minutes of the greatest road anxiety I had ever experienced, the road straightened and flattened. Vieste, an oasis of campgrounds, hotels, and restaurants, opened before us. She was calm, peaceful, and apparently oblivious of the great dangers that confronted those who sought her charms.

As happened so often during moments like this on the trip, Nancy was mostly silent. Rapt in the deepest concentration, she drove the car with the raw nerves of an Olympic bob sledder. Yet, as I loosened my grip from a courtesy handle in the car, I sensed a presence who many centuries before had guided the tiller on Odysseus' ship as it carved its way between Scylla and Charybdis.

CHAPTER 14

▼

THE WISDOM OF
TIRESIAS

Despite the example of the self-blinding of Oedipus, blindness does not represent a desired condition for human beings, yet it does come to many. Sometimes, as in my case, it comes slowly over decades. To others it comes suddenly, terrifyingly. Yet, throughout the ages there has been a sense that although much is lost in blindness, something also is given. At this point I'd like to recount my own sense of what I've gained through blindness and some tips on how a blind person might prepare for a long foreign journey.

The first benefit of blindness is the recognition that there are many, many caring people in the world. This is not sentimental rubbish. It's objective and experienced truth. In addition to Nancy, I have been assisted by hundreds of people since I lost my vision, some of them helping me at great inconvenience to themselves. Andy Haaland a colleague of mine, drives me to work every day and gladly makes personal stops I request to keep my life going. Lolly Carpenter and Bev Carey, the office secretaries, put themselves out to help me succeed. They have twenty other people to service, but they accept stress to help me. One day last week I counted nine separate individuals who helped me get through my day. I thank the gods for them. I also thank the gods that I have learned the basic premise of blind survival: one gains control by giving up control.

Once one has willingly given up the limiting tendency toward control and confidently embraced the compassion of others, a relatively full life is possible. When I received training on how to use a cane, I commented to my trainer that there couldn't be many blind people in Cortland because I never came across them. He sadly laughed and told me there were many blind people in the city: they just never left their homes.

There are, of course, reasons for this isolation. People are still ashamed of their imperfections and disabilities. Then there is the sheer terror for the blind of not knowing where one happens to be. I can assure the reader that to be outside the home and lose one's orientation sucks the rigidity from a person's bones. When this has happened to me, I can feel the sense of panic and dependency grow to nearly unbearable levels. And, remember, I have faith in people and have a fairly high sense of self-esteem and confidence. What must this be like to some others!

Yet, there really is no choice for the blind. They have to be encouraged to get out, to cope, to live. I remember that old trust exercise people would do where a person would fall backward and a friend would catch the person and prevent the fall. The blind have to take the risk to trust.

Once this occurs and the coping process begins, blindness will reveal some advantages. First, I noticed I became a much better listener. Since the oral and aural parts of communication largely supplanted reading and writing, I had to become a better listener. And, since most sighted people are awful listeners (research points to about 25% efficiency), I was able to develop a strength in a needed area where the sighted were weak. Indeed the need to be listened to is so great that people would want me around to listen to their story or would ask me to recount what happened at a meeting we both attended since I had heard the proceedings more effectively.

Another aspect of the blind person as listener is that the speaker's appearance evaporates as a factor of communication. I find that this is terribly important in my communication with females. As far as I can tell, males send out body language and other non-verbal signals to females based upon the age and attractiveness of the female. Some of these signals are subtle, some aren't. Whatever they are, women feel them very strongly and put up with them as part of the usual female-male communication process.

However, when females talk to me, age and looks are not elements of the communication. I respond to the voice tones and content of the communication. In other words I am more attuned to the spirit and soul of the woman. I am not pre-conditioned by what I see. When I respond to the youthful exuberance of a woman in her mid 60s, she somehow is getting a communication response she may not have experienced for forty years. Some women I have discussed this with talk about the liberating nature of the communication.

Another factor is that since I am blind, women don't have to worry about me in any physical sense. Since I am not seen as a physical threat, they reduce the limits of the social space they usually maintain around males. I quickly become like a family member. This sexual spacing reduction was one of the pleasant surprises of my blindness. Indeed, because I listen to them in a special way and present an unusual kind of male accessibility, women often like to be around me. It's no wonder that jealous males often call my cane a "chick stick." Fortunately for me, Nancy understands the source of the attraction and allows me to enjoy this facet of my blindness.

Another benefit of blindness is that I don't have to see what is unpleasant. On a fishing trip into Canada several years ago, the black flies were in the millions. One of my companions was so upset by this flying infestation that he nearly had a nervous breakdown. However, as

I ate my lunch I was hardly bothered although I did not remember using raisin bread to make my sandwich.

On our travels I have not been put off by the tawdriness of the cheaper accommodations we may have selected. As a result I'm perfectly happy in a bargain. I also know that Nancy is always vigilant about health matters, so I need not be concerned that what I don't see will hurt me.

Another comment about blindness in general is that it gives one a competitive advantage, not a disadvantage. Whenever a blind person does something done in the sighted world such as writing a piece, singing a song, cooking a dinner, or giving a speech, people see the blind person doing the activity blindfolded, and it becomes somehow wonderful, even if sight is not the primary requisite for the task. In fact, sometimes sight is a clear drawback. In public speaking, for example, vision leads to the development of a manuscript. This leads to reading a speech rather than performing it without notes. Since I'm blind, I never use notes in speeches. I rehearse my speeches like mad. When I give them, people react as if I'm walking on water.

Karaoke singing is another activity I do where vision is not necessarily a plus. Since I can't see the words, I don't look at them; I look in the direction of the audience and perform the song. Although my repertoire is limited to songs I know, those songs are very effective because they are performed and not recited.

The final advantage I will speak of is the usefulness of blindness in keeping us humble. In Greek tragedy the hero falls because of hubris, a kind of immoderate pride. In fact, the danger of such pride was so well known to the Romans that when a conquering general was given a triumphal parade through Rome, a slave was placed in the chariot to keep reminding the general he was only human and he shouldn't let the triumph go to his head. Those of us who are blind have this blindness for our slave as we ride our chariot through life. It's hard to be proud and arrogant after I've brushed my teeth with skin cream, or cooked blueberries when I thought I was cooking peas or walked into a corner where there was no doorway. It's impossible to be pompous when I flip my pancakes and miss the griddle or pour milk over my cereal until it overflows. Day in and day out I am reminded I am only human.

Yet, this is where a sense of humor becomes invaluable. In its way what happens is funny. It's often surprising and usually quite incongruous with the professional role I hold in my job. I thank the gods I don't have that gravitas that was so bandied about in the last presidential election. That quality would make me look like a pathetic fool.

Thus far, I've commented on general suggestions for coping with blindness: appreciating the compassion of others and giving up control, taking the risk of getting out in the world, and recognizing that blindness provides opportunities as well as its disadvantages. I'd like to end these general thoughts with an image I find useful although it is not new by any means. This image involves playing the cards that life has dealt us. Each of us gets a hand full of different qualities with varying levels of privilege or pain. In my hand I have mostly good cards. I'm intelligent—perhaps a queen or a king. I'm told I'm relatively good-looking, especially for a guy in his mid-fifties—let's say a jack. I can sing well—a queen. I have a fine sense of humor—my ace. Then there's my vision. Well, since I was sighted at one time, let's say this is a four or five. In any event, I've been dealt some good cards. Now, I can whine about the vision card, or I can play my hand. Most card players will tell those who ask to play the cards that have been dealt, not to dream about cards that aren't there. Dealing with blindness works the same way. One can try to cope or one can fold. People who fold lose, and no other cards are dealt. People who play their good cards can, if they play these cards well enough, win beyond their wildest dreams.

For those who want to win at the game of life, foreign travel may be worth a play. What would be the best course of action for someone seeking to go abroad with a disability like blindness?

First, you should anticipate the experience. After identifying the general locations you wish to visit, securing a companion, and preparing a budget, begin learning about the history, culture, and geography of the places you would like to visit. I'd recommend starting this six to nine months before the date of travel. Recordings for the blind, books on tape, and conversations with your companion can all be useful here. As you learn more about an area, certain specific places will become important to you.

Next, set up an itinerary. Don't be too ambitious. There will always be much more to visit and learn when you get to your locations than you actually know about when you are planning.

Next, pack sanely. As a blind person you don't want to have so many bags that they can get out of the control of you and your companion. Think about how you would guard your possessions while your partner wandered off to get the rental car. Even if you can carry all your belongings for a short distance, you might have to set things down if a long or steep walk is involved.

Next, think about your expectations for each location. What do you expect from each site? Are you looking for tastes and smells? The feel of the place by foot travel? Are you interested in tape tours? In historical and cultural readings by your companion?

You should also consider how you will keep yourself amused when your companion takes a break from you or goes to an attraction independently. In my trips I like to have a portable cassette player and a pocket short-wave radio with headphones. In this way I can spend hours of time by myself without becoming impatient. I've also gotten quite good at killing time in cafés and bistros. Occasionally quite interesting conversations will develop. Eavesdropping can also be fun. In any case your companion can help you decide if the place is friendly and secure.

After each day you might want to develop a way to digest your experience. Will you keep a taped or written log? I find that either method helps to highlight special experiences and sharpen insights.

Finally, the experience of travel is a life-changing and life-affirming event, but it is not necessarily a 24/7 party. The more ambitious and potentially rewarding the trip, the more likely that a few things will go wrong—sometimes significant things. Don't think of yourself as a tourist; think of yourself as an important character in a novel. This will lessen your sense that you should always be pampered. There will be down moments but these will pale against the life-affirming vibrancy of the entire experience.

Lastly, as a postscript to my comments for the blind, I would just add that an e-mail address where you can receive messages and a few credit cards appropriately validated so you can use foreign ATM's will go a long way to keeping you secure and happy. My chapter on Hermes has shown you some of the downsides of modern technology.

In summary, blindness is not the end of the world, but the ends of the world are in reach for those who believe in others, believe in themselves, and believe in what is possible.

CHAPTER 15

▼

THE BARD'S BEST

As I near the conclusion of my tale I can't help but think of the oral singer, the bard, who might once again bring those places alive that I visited with the greatest of enjoyment and pleasure. Like Odysseus in the court of Alcinous, I would send the singer of songs a choice cut of meat and a bowl of wine if he would let me hear again of the wonders of my favorite places.

Indeed, the readers of this story are certainly curious about what I, a blind traveler have etched in my memory. Indeed, often-asked questions of any traveler are "What did you like best?" or "What would you go back to again?"

I will, therefore, give my top ten places to revisit if the gods so blessed me and Athena willed it. Obviously, there are places that would always reward revisitation: Athens, Rome, Florence, Venice, etc. These are fabled cities, rich enough in culture, history and artistic treasure to repay visits for a lifetime. Here, I would like to name lesser-known places but sites still wonderful in their own way as places I'd like to visit again as well as recommend to other travelers for their inspection.

TOP TEN PLACES TO REVISIT

10. Aquitermé

Situated in hills not too far from Genoa, this small city possesses both cultural and recreational treasures in a comfortable and stress-free setting. The remains of a Roman aqueduct, fully illuminated at night, can be seen by the partially sighted. One of Italy's largest swimming pools offers refreshment and resort excitement in summer months. I recall this city as a place where prices were reasonable and where I could slow down a bit from the frenetic pace of tourist travel in the larger urban areas.

9. Naoussa

More a town than a city, Naoussa is at the other end of the Greek Island of Paros from the main harbor. The island is small, so the bus ride is relatively short. Even if the distance were longer, the ride would be well worth it. The place is wonderfully charming and contains a fine variety of cafes and restaurants along its narrow pedestrian walkways. The unsighted can walk fairly freely without much concern for any traffic. In addition, the food is good, and bargains can be had. I enjoyed a wonderful gyro and beer while sitting at one of the two tables on the street belonging to the tiniest of restaurants.

8. Paestum

A bit too far south of Rome for some, Paestum features some wonderful archeological remains from the Magna Graecia period and later (600-400 B.C.). At night the temples are illuminated, making a fine view for diners in the restaurants that border the archeological site. Although Paestum itself is rather run-down and has a honky-tonk resort ambience, the beach is fine, and there are pockets of good restaurants and very pleasant cafes.

7. Nafplion

Its three fortresses, proximity to Mycenae and Argos, and seaside location commend this city to any tourist. For me, a desire to go back is kindled by memories of its many, many small restaurants. For someone with visual problems, the tastes and smells of Nafphion combine for a real treat.

6. Siena

Going to a medieval city is one thing; going to a medieval city that is still alive is quite another. Siena still lives. Although I have already been there twice, I would not mind going back to walk its cobblestoned streets and hear those echoes bouncing against walls and buildings that have stood in constant use for so many centuries. During the day I dined and drank beneath the Tuscan sun in cafes surrounding the city's great plaza. At night I followed the Corpus Christi procession that wound through the ancient streets on the way to a chant-filled cathedral.

5. Taormina

Even if one is blind, the lofty position of this magnificent site is engaging. The cable car ride up to the town and the sea breezes rising a thousand feet intoxicate all who visit this marvelous place. Although the blind may not see Mt. Etna proclaiming its smokey presence beyond the walls of the great theater, the intrepid blind tourist can climb the stairs and sit on stone benches that have supported theater-goers for over 2300 years.

4. Segesta

If one has any sight left, he should get to Segesta in Sicily as soon as possible. The well-preserved Greek temple is set on a dark hillside that provides a great background for viewing the temple on a sunny Mediterranean day. Viewed from the opposite hillside with brilliant wildflowers exploding from the ground all around, this brilliant temple will convince even the most skeptical that the gods do indeed exist.

3. The Gargano Promontory—Vieste

Something of a combination of Big Sur, Cape Cod, and the Adirondacks, the Gargano Promontory juts out into the Adriatic Sea as a spur on the Italian boot. Rugged and beautiful, it has the city of Vieste as its easternmost point. Although the promontory is out of the way and the trip to Vieste is tiring and taxing, I hope to get there again. The area has sandy beaches and a wide variety of accommodations including four-star campgrounds with every conceivable style of bungalow, fine restaurants on the beach, and large swimming pools with bar. With Nancy I was able to enjoy swimming in both salt and fresh water as well as participating fully in the pleasures of beach life.

2. The Italian Lake District

Lakes and snow-capped mountains in the background are magic. Indeed, they are visual narcotics. Even though I wasn't able to see this addictive combination at all hours of the day, when the sun's angle was right and when the haze had cleared just enough, the sight I beheld was adequate payment for any eye strain I had suffered. When I recall the resort amenities of the lakes—Garda, Como, Lugano, and Maggiore, I feel just like such classic Romans as the poet Catullus, who just couldn't get enough of the place and built a vast villa on Lake Garda to try to satisfy his addiction to this beauty.

1. Sounion

To be at Sounion at the tip of the Attic Peninsula In Greece is to feel the power of a god transformed into topographical features. In the shadows and shapes of limited vision one can sense the power of the place. In my visit I was able to see the remains of temples outlined against the muscular headlands as the wine-dark sea below concealed the form of Poseidon while his chilling breath blew across my body.

The path to Poseidon's temple was a bit rough but manageable, and the experience of being there was spiritually and emotionally exhilarating. I had no doubt why the builders had chosen to create a temple there.

These, then, are the ten places that I'd revisit in a minute. Each possesses special qualities that even I as a blind man could appreciate. Sometimes, as I indicated earlier, it is the very blindness that perhaps made a place special. In Paestum, for example, I felt a much stronger connection to the place than either Nancy or Nick. While both enjoyed the ruins, the restaurants, our hotel, and the beach, they were put off by the economic deterioration they saw in the area. This background detracted from their enjoyment; it didn't affect mine.

Another place where my blindness acts as though I was wearing more than rose-colored glasses was the beach at Vieste on the Gargano Promontory. One day I am told the Adriatic was littered with paper plates, plastic bags, and other such items. Nancy reacted with disgust at this pollution. The next day when the wind direction shifted, the sea was clear. Nonetheless a visual impression had definitely settled in Nancy's mind.

Because of this I wonder if Nancy would ever drive across the promontory again. While I could feel the tension in the car and react to the G forces as the car twisted and turned to the contortions of the highway, Nancy could also see the dangers posed both by the road and by the oncoming cars. I doubt she would take such risks to swim among the litter she so vividly remembered.

Of course, there are places that didn't rise to the top of my list because of the difficulties my lack of vision caused. Delphi, for instance, is a spiritually wonderful place, but its congestion and uneven stairs make me pause about a second visit. Agamemnon's Palace at

Mycenae, a high point of my visit, offered such challenges and such possibilities for injury that I would require more motivation than I now possess to try it again. Similarly, the tour group mobs at Syracusa and Agrigento detracted from their positioning on my list of places I'd like to revisit.

Suffice it to say that I, like any traveler, am fickle. In fact I am even more so, for the objectivity perhaps encouraged by sight is replaced by subjective extrapolation of stimuli detected by my other senses. Nonetheless, what these senses tell me is real, and I can only hope that in some ways that this reality approaches truth.

EPILOGUE

▼

A few years ago a colleague of mine gave me a great compliment. He said, "Although Dan has vision problems, he can often see things hidden to others." Humbly, I accept this as a truth. In deciding to make this trip, I saw that the risks were worth the potential outcomes. I also saw that to do, to experience, is not something only for the sighted. Vision is just one of our senses; furthermore, thought and imagination transcend the sensory world. On this trip the people and culture of ancient civilizations came alive for me. I walked where Socrates had walked; I stood in Mycenae, and, like Orestes, pondered the actions of Clytemnestra. I passed through space where Spartans had marched toward Thermopylae; I strode in the Forum in Rome in Caesar's footsteps, enjoyed Hadrian's gardens in Tivoli, and spent a warm morning at Catullus' villa in Sirmione.

I also saw more clearly a presence that I have known for more than thirty-six years—my wife Nancy. In her mid-fifties and weighing less than 125 lbs., Nancy would not be a likely hero for an epic journey, but I think she was the hero of this one. She couldn't hurl a javelin very far or hold a sword very long, but in this trip she displayed a mental strength and courage that the Spartans and Romans would both admire.

I don't believe I lessen her achievement by suggesting that she had superhuman help in the person of Athena. The Athenians, after all, never felt the least bit lessened by giving full homage to this beautiful warrior goddess. Like the Athenians, Nancy and I are thankful for her aid.

0-595-27943-0